It's Hell Up

By J S Austin

Chapter One

"He's on his way, me Lord."

"Good. Is everything ready?"

"Yes, me Lord."

"Excellent."

Chapter Two

"You're dead mate," the Grim Reaper said in a chirpy sort of way.

"I'm sorry, who's dead? My name is Mr Zed Bartholomew Wallace. Not Mr Dead."

"No you pillock. You are dead. Zedrick Bartholomew Wallace of 145 Gill Road is dead. Look, that's you dead. The one on the floor with the sort of squashed look about him."

Zed had, up to this point, lived a relatively unexceptional existence. He enjoyed coasting through life avoiding excitement; or as Zed called it dangerous activities. Not born to be a great leader, nor having read at Cambridge, he lacked any athletic prowess and preferred lifting pints to lifting weights at the gym. If you questioned him on mankind's greatest achievements, he would simply reply: "Beer." He'd probably bore you with his philosophical theories: God couldn't possibly exist; no one would be so cruel as to create the hangover. But that is neither here nor there, as at this present time Zed was struggling with a rather more perplexing issue. Why was there a man in black, holding a scythe, looking at him in a strangely unsettling, yet friendly way? Was it a Halloween costume? No, that was over two months ago. Or had he spent a touch too much money on this rather amazingly realistic Grim Reaper outfit? Even more puzzling, why could he see himself looking deader than a stuffed dodo after colliding with a stampeding herd of overweight elephants? Luckily the Halloween obsessed man helped him out. "You're dead mate," the Grim Reaper repeated.

Zed mustered up all his grey, red and blue brain cells to review the evidence his accuser had laid before him. He walked around the squashed vision of himself and admitted that things were looking bad.

Leaning down he stretched out a tentative arm to pat the motionless chest. At the point of contact, where the arm should feel the soft flesh of the chest, he felt nothing! Instead his arm carried onto where his heart had once pumped so freely. It was at this point Zed's brain caught up with reality and abruptly switched off.

The Grim Reaper was perplexed. His job was to lead souls to the afterlife. He was not paid, (nor insured), to carry one there and he was damned if he would start now. He was pretty sure souls could not faint. Hoisting Zed over his shoulder the Grim Reaper cursed and muttered something about "souls these days" and "no respect for their elders" and 'being older than time itself …..".

Chapter Three

"Get up you lard-arsed son of a bitch before I get a Jehovah's Witness to bore you awake."

"Oh hell, I'm in hell," thought Zed looking up to see a tall angry man shouting tempestuously in his face. His brain, having accepted death, assumed he must now be in the afterlife. (It's amazing how the human brain possesses an almost instantaneous acceptance of death. Few brains refuse to acknowledge their demise - and they end up trapped between dimensions as ghosts.)

Zed got to his feet and looked around. It certainly didn't look like hell. The ground resembled fluffy clouds and the sky was postcard blue. Pleasingly, he noted the lack of rivers flowing with lava or souls scorched by fire.

After a brief moment of panic, his senses fine-tuned themselves to their new environment and he made a closer inspection. Underneath the white substance he'd assumed was heavenly cloud forming a majestic floor, he now saw what looked and smelled more like the smoke from a cheap disco machine, billowing over a rather grim looking parquet floor. The sky was still perfectly blue but somehow didn't look real. Trying to make sense of the view from his eyes, he was knocked for six by a booming voice.

"Stop pissing in the air and get in the queue!"

"Excuse me Mr..."

"Saint to you, you guttersnipe. I am Saint Peter."

"Ar Mr..."

"Watch it!"

"Saint Peter, I'm in heaven then. Splendid."

"You ain't yet and if you don't join that queue quicker than lightning strikes you never will be."

Zed gawked in the direction Saint Peter was indicating with his finger. All around there were hundreds of queues all leading to the same gate.

"Is that the gate to heaven?"

"Course it friggin is, you muppet."

Zed tried not to act too surprised by what he saw; this Peter chap seemed a bit tetchy.

"Just well er it looks like a small wooden garden gate. I was expecting a larger, more golden affair - perhaps in a smudge more impressive sort of style."

"Well yes, we had to sell that one to cover our costs and this gate was going cheap. And it does the job perfectly adequately thank you very much."

"I see. So which queue do I join?"

"Religion?"

"Pardon?"

"What was you sodding religion, and don't be a smartass and say Jedi."

"I believed in peace and harmony."

"Hippy ass. Nationality?"

"British."

"Ok. Then see that queue there where everyone is trying to act polite? That's your queue."

Depressingly the queue snaked seemingly for miles moving in a shuffle rather than a rush.

"Why can't I go in that one where everyone is going through really quickly?"

"No, no. That's for the Germans; efficient even in death. Just be glad you're not Italian. See that queue there; the one where everyone is arguing and barging. That's the Italians. Takes a whole week to shout your way through that. Now get in line and I'll see you at the gate."

Obeying the Saint, Zed hurried off in a slow sort of hurry to his designated queue. All around him people wandered, some in a daze, others desperately trying to work out where to go.

Joining the long British queue, Zed stared up at the sky, daydreaming. This is atrocious thought Zed. I'm in heaven and having to queue. He took a big intake of breath and expelling it in a long, loud, thoughtful manner.

"I knew I had the right religion."

Zed tentatively looked round to see who was so rude as to strike up a conversation; the last thing he wanted was a chat. He found a strange, awkward man looking overly excited. Short, chubby, with ridiculously large round glasses for such a small head, he appeared far too happy. Never trust an overly happy person was one of Zed's key life mottos. He reminded Zed of characters he'd spent his life avoiding.

"Yes, very nice," Zed replied attempting to end the conversation at that. He was not in the mood for chitchat, especially not with this weirdo.

The man carried on regardless. "My name's Bob." He waited for a response and again received none. "This is stupendous. Who knew that the church of Ehud the Left-Handed commanded so many followers."

"The what? I'm not an Ehud the Left-Handed church member. I'm not left handed and who is Ehud?"

The short man looked flabbergasted. "Then why are you in heaven? You should be in hell you blasphemous pig!"

"From what I can tell old chap most religions have got in. Even the ones that didn't believe like me." Bob looked crushed and Zed gave him a smile with the satisfaction of knowing he had made no effort to get here while this rude little man had spent his life wasting it.

"You mean I've resisted the temptation of women, prayed every day and have even resisted the urge to put a stumbling block behind a blind person. Ever since I read the law in the Avodah Zarah the temptation has been there."

"You never know, God may get you a better room for being good." Zed's brain took a few seconds but eventually caught up.

"What did you say about blind people?"

"You know. It is commanded that we should..."

"Yes, yes, I heard. But not tripping up the blind I think is the case in general, not just in your religion."

Seriously, this guy had to resist attacking innocent blind people and he still gets into heaven. What other loonies did they allow in?

For twenty more terrible minutes Zed had to endure general chat on this and that and of how Bob had never eaten Ma'aser Sheni oil outside Jerusalem, and hundreds more ludicrous laws he had lived by.

Remembering a quote from his old religious education classes, "for the evil doers shall be cut off, but those who wait for the Lord shall inherit the land," he wondered if it referred to the waiting in queues up here in heaven. And as it happened, he was now at the front.

"Yes Zed my man."

"Oh hello. That is hello Saint."

It was Peter.

"Says here that my man has done some shit that would make the Devil cringe. Begs the question bredwin why let you in?"

Shock crippled Zed momentarily. He'd not considered that he would be interrogated at the gates. His brain recognised at this point that it best act fast else the brain may be extracted and painfully sent to hell.

"I don't mean to offend you, your Sainthood, but could you possibly have got one or two facts wrong. I'm sure my life has had a few hiccups along the way - cheating and minor theft or two - but I've read the bible and I'm sure there is a clause about forgiveness and whatnot."

Zed was not brave arguing with a man of Peter's power. No, he was just a stupid man who went through life knowing things will work themselves out.

"You arguing with me, bitch?" All of a sudden Peter seemed to grow ten feet high and looked, one would say, angry. "Are you or are you not Hitler?"

"What! No, no, no. I'm not Hitler. Honest. Look - no dodgy moustache or general evil look. I'm Zedrick Bartholomew...."

Quickly returning to normal size Peter double-checked his list. "Oh yeah man. Says here that you were a general pussy that went through life being a goody-goody. In you go asshole."

Zed had been forced to read the bible in his youth and was pretty sure language like that was not acceptable in heaven.

Saint Peter watched Zed walk through the gates and had a little giggle. "Gets them every time that Hitler gag."

Chapter Four

"What do you mean: he's in the queue to heaven?" Two red fiery eyes stared accusingly at the messenger. They portrayed anger and evil more vividly than words ever could.

Chapter Five

Passing through the garden gates of heaven was something Zed decided to savour. It meant he'd made it. His life had built up to this moment. Yes, he didn't believe in it nor deserve it but he was here now and would bloody well enjoy it.

With his chest pumped out and feeling like a million dollars, he marched through the (not-so-great) gate of heaven. He paused, half expecting cheers and high fives from all around, but instead he saw stretched in front of him a worn, stained, red carpet with a contrasting, freshly mown lawn either side. Birds were tweeting but Zed could only hear their song; he could not see them. A large neon light, flashing 'Welcome to Heaven - Congratulations', hung from what looked like fake clouds. Soothing music played its annoying vibes.

Heaven, as everyone knows, is a dreamland - something beyond our imagination. It is perfection, a fairy tale, an indescribable beauty. Yet what he saw in front of him was rather deflating. For some who have lived their life for this moment the phrase 'burst one's bubble' would understate their disappointment.

A living human brain would find this situation difficult to process - a whiff on the detrimental side. Many have theorised on the possibility of an overloaded brain exploding. Zed now found himself like the rat in an experiment that could cement theory into fact.

But to his dead brain this sort of thing was allowed. The brain becomes much more accepting of strange and mysterious events. (Some may say the brain was smoking the pipe from whence the neon sign came; it relaxes a bit when dead.) Zed's brain stirred, it was experiencing another side effect from the green herb, hunger.

"Well this is a trifle whacky. Do I need food when I'm dead?" Zed knew that in southern USA they loved their soul food. Perhaps now in heaven, and no longer technically speaking a human but a soul, fried chicken and macaroni cheese would be the staple diet. "I could live with that as long as there's beer to wash it down with."

"Wait up, wait up."

It was that annoying dweeb from the queue.

"What ho, here you are again. Well best be off."

Still smiling and generally looking annoying, he exclaimed: "Yes we had, hadn't we sire. Where are you taking me?"

"Well I'm going to go see what they do for food round these parts as my belly is rumbling more than my gran's old tumble dryer. What do you mean, 'we' and 'sire'?"

"Oh sure. I saw how you talked to Saint Peter and I knew only one man would ever do that,"

"And he is?"

"Well you know. The One. It is written. So I shall follow you to the ends of the earth. I mean heaven."

There is a type of human, commonly known as an idiot who is desperate to follow. This is the DNA of all cults. There are idiots who are desperate to follow and an inflated ego who is desperate to be followed (and on the side become rich). Here we have a gullible 'groupie' who wants to follow someone – Zed; but Zed being the opposite of the accepted "followed" type showed no intentions to lead.

Zed's brain couldn't grasp this nonsense but there was no point arguing as the guy could, for all he knew, be a psycho killer. "Let's just take him to lunch and do a bunk when he goes to the toilet," thought Zed.

"What was your name again?"

"Bob."

"I shall call you Dumbo. Much more fitting."

So off they went following the tatty red carpet, under the neon sign and out into a throng of hustle and not forgetting bustle of activity. One could only imagine the wonders they might find. What they actually found was a market square on a humongous scale. The cobbled floor was awash with hundreds of people, and they all seemed to be selling something.

"You sir, welcome to heaven," said a pleasant yet unnerving woman, thrusting a flyer into Zed's hand.

Zed scanned the leaflet.

'Heaven. Mormons were right. Below is how you should act in our Mormon heaven....'

"Leave him alone, you blasphemous whore," said an old, nun-looking nun. "Here take this and adhere to it."

'So you made it to heaven. You must be catholic. Good choice....'

Not having time for religious blathering, Zed only had one thing on his mind. "Excuse me, mad women of varying religious beliefs but could you point me in the general direction of a pub with good beer and even better food?"

"Beer in heaven? If you look here, point three on our leaflet, alcohol is strictly outlawed in Mormon heaven."

"No beer?"

"Well there's the Bull and Spear just round that corner but God will forsake anyone who goes in."

"Well, I will enjoy my forsaking as long as they do beer. Thank you strange woman."

Zed, being of average height, well dressed and who spoke in a nonchalant, charming, yet apathetic way, could come across as rude when uninterested in the conversation. Walking off, both women hissed something that in their religions was banned.

Indeed, just around the corner stood an English style pub, and Zed wasted no time in ordering his first drink in heaven.

Many a new heavener supped their first ale in the Bull. From doctors to shoe shiners, firemen and priests, all have sighed a huge sigh of relief; heaven permits the sweet nectar that is alcohol. Ordering two drinks, Zed and Bob sat down on a tatty sofa. Its leather cushions could boast for hours about the famous buttocks that had graced its form but Zed's and Bob's were not some it wanted to remember.

"Sire. Are you saying the mighty one has changed his opinion on alcohol?"

"Just drink this Dumbo and then tell me if anyone would not allow it. Bottoms up."

"I was never allowed to think about bottoms up," Bob thought out loud.

Chapter Six

The Beast, Lucifer, Satan, The Antichrist, Prince of Darkness, or whatever you may call him was not happy. The bringer of darkness, creator of evil, ruler of the underworld and all round bad chap sighed a huff of frustrated anger.

The Devil was normally quite a tolerant and polite thing but recently he'd grown angry. Trying the normal stress release technique of torturing a few souls early this morning to calm himself down proved not as effective as usual. All he had asked for was to make sure Zed be sent to hell. Staring into a golden-framed, wall-to-floor mirror he let out a roar of anger, a roar of such power the foundations of hell vibrated. The consequences of Zed staying in heaven were unthinkable as his many advisors on the subject had reminded him time and again. In fact he was due another meeting with them soon and was not very much looking forward to it.

Chapter Seven

An old form teacher from Zed's youth, Mr Hepworth - who coincidently was currently being harshly treated in the fires of hell - had once remarked that Zed was on course to waste his life away drinking in pubs. And to be fair, he was quite right. Zed would be quick to point out though that Sir was not as clever as he thought. He neglected to foretell that Zed would drink his death away in heaven as well. Judging from the brief evidence, this might also be true.

Like on earth, no matter where you travel, you can never escape the English. Anglicising wherever they land, the English do not care for change and have no thoughts of adapting to "their" way. The first rule of conquering a land without an army is to set up the traditional English pub. The checklist for any want-to-be landlord launching such a colonial attack is:

England flags proudly hung on as many walls as possible.

Dartboard with broken darts and no chalk

Pool table preferably stained from beer

Fruit machines

Full English breakfast served till midday

Only the Irish have invaded more territories with their friendlier, atmospheric, Guinness laden pubs.

The Bull, being an English establishment, greatly helped Zed feel at home. After Bob succeeded in ripping the pool table cloth, landing a dart in a not-so-happy drinker's nether regions and generally acting in an embarrassing way, Zed attempted to get a few moments to himself.

Having spent the last hours ordering drink after drink, Zed found himself alone in the corner of the pub and started to think. "I'm in heaven, which is good. But I'm alone which is bad."

On Earth, Zed had been a bachelor and enjoyed his social life immensely. Not one to actively look for friendship, he somehow acquired a large amount of friends, something he never really understood and occasionally cursed when wanting to be left to himself. He rarely felt alone having a large social group to call upon whenever needed. On quiet nights in, with a bottle of wine, his loving dog Jennings willingly obliged by keeping Zed company on the sofa. But now realisation dawned on him that here he was by himself in heaven, no one to pop to the pub with, to moan about the cricket to, or meet in his favourite coffee house for an overpriced latte.

His parents passed away some years ago and being an only child on earth there was no family - just much loved friends.

Suddenly there it was. A light bulb illuminated Zed's head, flashing on and off, shouting eureka. "Maybe my mum and dad are in heaven," thought Zed. The idea burst into Zed's brain and burnt brightly. Not metaphorically but actually burnt. A yelping sound was expelled from his mouth and he scratched his mop of a hairstyle thoroughly to sooth his head.

Zed's brain, being a pessimistic type, promptly dampened the flames with a counter thought. "But I have no idea where they would be. Come to think about it how big is heaven, what is the public transport system like and do they have the yellow pages?"

While alcohol works its way in and around the body, thoughts that normally would be dismissed as ridiculous take on a whole new meaning. Zed's brain had mentioned his parents and the alcohol grabbed these words and made them into a mission that, without fail, must be completed and started straight away.

Well after his next pint anyway.

Chapter Eight

Waking up in heaven for the first time is a surreal experience. Add a hangover to the equation and it becomes soul destroying - that is, if your soul can be destroyed once in heaven. As it is the soul that goes to heaven, if destroyed, would something else go to another heaven? Should spectacle-clad boffins be colliding souls around the large hadron atom smasher thingy to work this out? Anyway, we've digressed. Hangovers to Zed had proved God didn't exist so to have one now in heaven verified one fact: God detests drinkers.

The foul taste of cigars crushed and dried in atrociously foul air for a thousand years lingered inside Zed's mouth, a clear sign of a good night. Rolling, stumbling and panicking, Zed fell out of bed and onto his boney behind. No shouts of pain, just some bemused grunting noises acknowledged the fall.

It's about this time that the brain began asking questions. Zed's eyes, although open already, only now started working. They answered his first pressing question; yes he had slept in what appeared to be a hotel room, not a bad looking one at that. A double bed with luxurious cream covers, a scattering of cushions and a soft beige carpet which Zed was now familiarising himself with.

Other pressing questions were queuing to be answered but were outflanked by the need for water and a feeling of the imminent expulsion of sick. Making a dash for the bathroom, both tasks were accomplished one after the other, just in the wrong order. Toothpaste and brush were thoughtfully provided and Zed set about ridding his mouth of this sewage taste.

"You ok there, Zed?"

Zed spat the toothpaste out his mouth, spinning round frantically ready to defend himself. It did not occur to him that someone else shared the room.

"Oh it's you Bob." Relieved and yet also more on edge with this suspected psychopath so close, he finished the task of bleaching his mouth and returned to the bedroom to see if by any chance Bob had left. He had not.

"Refreshed now sire?"

"Yes, all tip top now and ready to find my parents."

The bit about his parents surprised himself even as he was saying it. Normally a plan made while drunk is quickly forgotten in the morning. But for some reason the thought of meeting his parents was firmly burnt, nailed and glued into his mind.

"Oh," Bob's voice radiated disappointment. "Are you not planning on finding some followers first and maybe, you know, preach and tell us what to wear and what food we can eat?"

Focusing on Bob, Zed felt annoyed. The man clearly has no hangover and looked as though he'd been up from the crack of dawn no doubt performing early morning stretches or other hideously dweebish activities.

"Look matey, what is it with all this dribble? If I were a suspicious chap I would think you mistook me for someone else."

"You are our saviour and leader," Bob said with unwavering conviction of someone who knows they are right and given conclusive proof they are wrong, would still know they are right.

Zed half joking replied: "Then I command you to go away and do whatever you want."

And with that, to Zed's surprise, he did. Without even a bye he was off.

"What a loony!"

Now he was alone, Zed sat down and thought. He had made up his mind that he would try to find his parents. 'Hang on,' his brain thought about saying. It considered debating the pros and cons of finding them and then got bored, so accepted that finding them seemed a logical thing to do.

But how to find them? If heaven contained every person that had ever died minus the naughty ones being eternally spanked in hell, then heaven must be large. No, not large - stupendously, mind-numbingly, behemothically large.

Map! Any good ex-Boy Scout would think of that. So up he got and after a quick freshen up he went down to reception to ask for a map and see how he could pay for this room.

Chapter Nine

Around a hexagonal (the most evil of all the shapes) iron table - which legend tells was cast with the five most demonic, black-hearted, degenerate humans to exist within the table itself - sat several men and women of varying ages, all in business suits from different eras, all looking rather ridiculous. Amongst them was one much larger and noticeably redder fella.

"Evening gentlemen," barked the Devil. "Let's open this meeting on point one, the failure to obtain Zed."

Back in the unorganised origins of hell, agendas and meetings were unheard of. Many millennia later and the Devil started organising meetings, which, if examined, were essentially shouting matches. After years of training he could now run a smooth meeting with agendas and even minutes – although they were taken down frantically in fear of a missed point resulting in a lost finger or two.

"Now I understand Mr Taylor has gone over the events that led up to this unfortunate failure and has a full root cause analysis. Please can you tell us all your findings and explain what went wrong."

Shuffling his prepared notes and looking overly confident Mr Taylor proceeded. "Well me Lord, the plan was simple."

"So you led me to believe."

"And it failed on the first part. He was supposed to go to purgatory but due to circumstances we have never seen before that boney one with a scythe carried him straight to heaven."

"So what was the contingency plan if your simple plan went wrong?"

Starting to look worried, Mr Taylor carried on. "There... there was no contingency plan. The plan was fool proof."

"Yet it went wrong," the Devil said slowly keeping direct eye contact with Mr Taylor. "So to put it simply, the plan was not fool proof?"

Starting to stutter a bit Mr Taylor answered: "Yes, suppose so."

"That's enough Mr Taylor. Please sit down."

The Devil had recently been on several project management courses always looking to improve himself and knew what was needed now.

"So who here has a plan B?"

Chapter Ten

Dingggg

Ding, ding, ding.

"I say, hello. Anyone there?"

Feeling mildly more alive, Zed's attempts to gain the attention of someone who worked at the hotel were proving futile. Everywhere seemed empty. On the way down from his room for the night, Zed failed to bump into a single soul and now found the reception desk unmanned. Growing more and more frustrated he gave the reception bell some punishment with a hard slap.

Dingggg.

Not expecting a response he stumbled back in shock as, without warning, smoke poured out from behind the reception desk and lights flashed from above. Mystic music filled the air – the type piped through badly run Indian restaurants - and then, with a burst of light, a woman in pure white robes with the not-standard-for-humans addition of wings appeared, as if from nowhere.

"Kneel down before me Zed, for I am your Lord and Saviour," she commanded with a powerful bass voice bouncing off all four walls, echoing each word with resounding dramatic effect.

Oh jeez. I've just dinged and annoyed God. I always knew He - I mean She - was female. Why else would men never be allowed to win an argument? Kneeling down in deep panic he heard giggling – and not in the way one would envisage God to laugh. Looking up tentatively, not knowing if custom allowed one to look God directly in the eyes, he was struck by what he saw and was a bit confused. God was doubled over in an uncontrollable state of laughter.

"Stand up Zed, I'm just the receptionist, Elemiah." Smiling at Zed with laughter just about under control, she still had the air of power about her.

Feeling both relief and disappointment, Zed, still wary that this could be God testing him, enquired politely: "But how did you know my name."

"I used thousands of years' experience, superior intellect - and also looked what name you were booked in under last night."

"Oh, silly me."

"You stumbled in just before I closed up for the night asking for the Yellow Pages and a room. You then proceeded to ask me if it hurt when I fell from heaven. After ten minutes of arguing about having never fallen from heaven, as I've always been in heaven, you went to bed."

Never that comfortable being with attractive women, Zed was turning a lovely shade of tomato.

"Oh, don't be embarrassed. I was flattered being chatted up by a guy like you. But I'm old enough to be your mother's mother's mother's mother's mother's ... You get the idea."

In life Zed had never settled down with a partner, and if you had ever heard some of his chat up lines to woo the ladies, you'd understand why.

"What's your name?" Zed asked cunningly, trying to avert the attention away from himself.

"I just told you silly, Elemiah. Heard of me down on earth?"

With the disappointment of not meeting God, Zed initially overlooked that currently he was chatting to an actual Angel. His brain quickly catching up and realising she could perhaps be rather important he checked.

"No, don't think so. Are you in the bible?"

"Oh, sort of. Never mind."

A nagging question had been forming in Zed's brain and it shot out before he could stop it.

"Can you fly?"

"Course I bloody can. Why else would I have wings? Admittedly God's first few attempts at wings on earth failed. Penguins, ostriches, squirrels were not such a success but up here our Angels' wings work wondrously."

Zed had by this time become more himself. "Well thanks for my room last night. It was most sporting of you to put me up. However I'm not sure how to pay you as my wallet's spirit did not rise with me."

"No need to pay, sweetie. In heaven we do not use money. All is free."

"Oh tremendous news." Zed remembered that he actually found this out last night when he didn't have to pay for any of his drinks. "Then can you help me? I must find my old man and mother but have no idea how."

Looking at this winged, tall, kind yet stern faced Angel, Zed had a feeling of stupidity. Should he ask about transport and Yellow Pages again or should he use his first meeting with a biblical Angel to ask a few questions about God? Having a lot of queries regarding the bible (he'd found parts a tad weird while learning about it at school) that could do with being answered. Why was God so against mixed fabrics for one thing?

"Well Zed, you first need to work out which part of heaven they live in."

"Which part? Is heaven not one continuous..", not certain on the word to use he settled on, "land mass?"

"Not quite. You see heaven's settlements are divided up into zones. The nature of who lives in the zones changes over the years but recently they appear to follow your earth centuries. After each earth century a new part of heaven is populated. So if you were the first person to die in a new century, you would enter through the gates to be greeted by no one. Just imagine getting to heaven and finding it empty? They must think, 'Am I the first non-sinner in history or is everyone just hiding?'. There's a map in the centre of the courtyard just outside this hotel that shows you the different zones. Once you work that out the only method of transport is to walk. God banned motorised vehicles twenty years ago. We think He thought, 'what's all the rush about; you have eternity to get to where you are going'."

This startling news shocked Zed to the core. Not the zone partitioning of heaven but its complete lack of transport. A stroll to the local pub yes, but any other reason for walking had eluded him for the last thirty-nine years. And now it seemed walking would be his eternal punishment for being allowed into heaven.

Angels of all the creeds have enhanced senses and can read a human's emotions pretty spot on. But she didn't require this skill with Zed. The look of terror and panic could be read on his face by a half-boiled French snail let alone an Angel of infinite years.

"You OK there, Zed?"

"Yes, yes, just you know, walking and all that."

"What do you mean dear?"

"Oh, I'm not a fan of the old walking stuff."

Elemiah laughed. "Get used to it. If you want to find your parents then walking is your only option. There are a few exceptions, like donkeys, but make peace with walking if you are serious about your journey."

"Yes, I shall find them", he said with a lot less vigour than the pre-walking news hour.

Feeling his enthusiasm melting away, he decided it was now or never if he was ever to heroically risk walking to find his parents.

"Well I must pop off now and find this great map."

"Nice meeting you, Zed. Something tells me we will meet again."

"Right, yes, what ho and off I go."

Zed tottered out bumping into a few chairs and doors on his way, still feeling the less desirable effects of a good night spent drinking.

Elemiah hurriedly closed up reception. She had a worrying feeling about Zed that she had never felt before and needed some reassurance or guidance on what she should do.

Chapter Eleven

The way the Devil talked changed greatly from century to century. Elocution lessons, public speaking courses, business talk, self learn audio books - he had tried them all. Always noticing that the most respected evildoers spoke in many ways, he was conscious of his limited vocabulary and aggressive manner. But when angered his old tone would slip back.

"Are you fucking for real? He has a follower already? And that meddling Angel has met him as well? If I was up there I'd have sorted this crap out in a fucking second. Seriously, I've the brains of every evil genius that ever lived at my disposal and more project managers than there are grains of sand, yet still this joke of a man wanders free. You know that when we have him, we will hold the key to all I – sorry, I mean 'we' - have ever wanted? Yet you fuck up time and time again. Right, get me someone to torture. I need to calm down."

"Right away your evilness, but we have news. Dantalion has infiltrated heaven and is currently on his way to find Zed." Scuttling off the servant heard the Devil shout after him.

"Just bring him here. You have 48 hours."

Little did the Devil know but at this moment Dantalion was frantically trying to explain to heaven's police why he was driving a Mustang V8 when clearly for the last twenty years all cars were banned.

Chapter Twelve

"What a dazzling place this is," Zed might have said walking out of the hotel if he were not still feeling the hangover blues. The courtyard that opened up outside the hotel bore a pleasingly close resemblance to the images dreamed about and conjured up when people described or imagined heaven. The floor sparkled with white marble - not your everyday run-of-the mill marble tiles but one complete, unbroken slab of marble covering the entire area; the type of marble only sold in heaven. Looking as if it were meant to be and having always stood there in the centre of the courtyard, spraying pearl blue water twenty feet high, was a wondrous fountain depicting Adam and Eve dancing round the paradise of heaven's garden, captured in such a way that made the scene feel almost real. Many who have seen this fountain have come to the same conclusion that in front of them lay the mystical legend of the fountain of youth. Stripping off they would rush in, covering their bodies with the water that grants eternal youth, and rushing out cold, wet and still old they'd begrudgingly put their clothes back on and mope off somewhere to dry.

Four large entrances into the courtyard were formed by stone arches, each with exquisitely detailed carvings of cherubs doing cheruby type things, and peppered around the marble floor statues of such beauty, that no man could possibly have created, danced their motionless dance.

The sky was again glistening blue with hardly a cloud in sight. Not many people were up and about as it was still quite early in the morning. Only the sound of the fountain's water disturbed the quietness of the courtyard. Ever blind to details, Zed had not noticed much of this with his banging headache taking up most of his attention. However, the headache failed to hamper him locating the map in extra quick time, which to Zed was a proud achievement in his current state of mind.

The map hung in a gold-leafed covered frame on a stone-built wall. Not like one of your minute, pathetic, excuses for a map used by many tourist boards. Whoever commissioned this map, emphasised the word large. It was four times the size of your average renaissance painting and luckily not on a ceiling but on the wall.

After a good five minutes of attempting to read the map, he came to an important conclusion - one that had the potential to shatter the illusions and beliefs of many believers. Namely that Intelligent Design is load of old codswallop. Whoever came up with that pseudoscience idea needed to be brought to this map and to be shown that God cannot even intelligently design heaven's basic layout - let alone the intricate details of nature's most impressive creatures.

What could be seen clearly were the zones the Angel talked about. Like countries, heaven's zones had boundaries and each zone was carefully labelled with the century name. Well at least, recent centuries were anyway. At some point in history God seemed to have decimalised everything, as some of the older areas appeared to be of random time periods. Logically you would think that one time period would be next to the corresponding one, but no. Scientists have never truly created a machine that can produce random movement, but God obviously had when choosing where to put the next lot of his people. Luckily, like all great maps, there was a big arrow saying 'you are here'. Finding his dear old parents' resting place would take a jolly long time. On quick observation there seemed to be thousands and thousands of zones, which logically of course there should be.

All this had taken up most of Zed's brain power and only now had the eyes been allowed to ask the brain who that strange robed man was resting on a bench under the map.

"Howdy, old man. I didn't see you there. How are you today?"

Jumping up, like a ninja ready to strike, the man looked around frantically.

"Where are you? Can you not see I am meditating?" The guy looked two hundred years old and the way he had sprung up amazed Zed. Like a playful kitten he had flung himself off the floor but was now patting the air around him and moving less like young cat and more like an injured sloth.

"Oh my mistake. I just hoped you could help me with this map?" But as it was now plain to see, the man was blind so Zed doubted he could help.

"You think I can't help, don't you mate? Well I'll have you know, Jesus himself met me once on earth and said to me: 'You blind guides, who strain out a gnat and swallow a camel'."

Zed looked at the man confused.

"And we all know what he meant by that. That even though I am blind, I can find a gnat and can lead you anywhere like a camel. Personally I would have said 'find a needle in a haystack and lead you to water like an elephant' but the big J was always strange."

Zed wanted to point out that what Jesus meant was more about greed and not particularly complimentary.

"I am Azaar, but you can call me Map Man or Map Master or the Mapster."

"Right ho. So just a thought, would you know a thing or three about this map?"

"I know this map better than the Lord Himself."

"This is amazing luck! Could you help? I need to find the zone allocated to the people in the prior century to this one."

"You want to know do you?"

"Well yes, that's just what I asked."

"Well I'll tell you."

"Top man."

"As soon as you get me a bottle of wine."

Zed didn't even bother arguing. Jesus was obviously right with his comment, so a bottle of wine it was to be.

"Any chance chappy you know where I could acquire one?"

"Just there." Pointing across the road in a manner that suggested this request was a frequent occurrence.

A few minutes later Zed was handing the wine over and being shown where he needed to go. Azaar ran his old skinny fingers across the map locating where they were and then in a breath of air zigzagged it across the map speaking in double quick time ending in "and here is where you want to get to."

Trying to remember everything - or at least anything - Zed's brain admitted that none of what was said or shown still remained in memory.

"Any chance you can show me again please, and a bit slower. I'm not in the best of ways this morning."

"Sure. Not a problem. I'd love to show you again. My pleasure."

"Top man. I'm ready this time."

"Just you'll need to get me another bottle of wine. For expenses you understand."

Without a word, Zed turned and headed off, annoyed that this man had got into heaven.

Take two went better. The directions, to Zed's shock, were explained in a slow and clearly understandable way.

Thanking Azaar for the belated help Zed asked: "One thing puzzles me. Why did you demand bottles of wine when all is free in heaven?"

"I can never leave this map as I am the Mapster. Even for the necessities I have to stay here to guide all who come."

Zed decided against asking about his toilet arrangements.

Unfortunately, the strange gnat finding man had not been to school when miles or kilometres were introduced to the curriculum, so Zed still had no idea how far away his parents were or how long the journey could take. Well he knew in 'hands' but whose hands did they use to measure with? He did know that by luck he only had to pass one zone border and then find something called a snail hole to get to where he needed to go. Wandering off in the direction given, Zed went through the instructions in his head. When Azaar had explained they seemed so simple, now already they were seemingly tricky and easily forgettable.

Panicking slightly that all the directions crammed within his brain would be lost, Zed took action. Having a rare good idea he resolved to write down all he remembered. And where better to get a pen and paper than a pub. This killed two possums with one pebble as there was no telling how long this journey would be. So a swift drink to help him on the long trot he expected to have through heaven seemed a splendid idea. For all he knew there could be fewer than one pub every mile en route so best he thought to get one or two in while he could.

Chapter Thirteen

Dantalion had fond memories of holidaying in heaven. Quite the beach lover, hell lacked any blue flag beaches - mainly down to the blood and fire - but here in heaven, back in the good old days, he would drive his Mustang down to one of thousands that heaven had to offer. Annoyingly, since his promotion to Great Duke of Hell - which he now thought more of a curse than a blessing - he never seemed to find time for holidays. This task the Devil had thrust upon him seemed yet another time consuming annoyance at first. Then the idea came to him: once business was taken care of, a trip to the beach could be sneaked in. Beach and perhaps an ice cream too.

The day started well. First, he'd arrived in heaven alive. The many methods used by demons to access heaven are all filled with danger. Passing through a vortex - for want of a better word for an indescribable rip in the delicate fabric between heaven and hell - one in a hundred demons lose a limb or more en route. Secondly, finding his old Mustang still glistening from the wax that was lovingly buffed into the bodywork some thirty years ago, on his last visit, pleased him greatly. And seeing no one had attempted to steal it even though the keys were there on full view in the ignition both delighted and confused him in equal measures.

Being a convertible that was forever topless, Dantalion vaulted over the door in a 'I'm so cool, look at me, sort of way'. He knew nothing could go wrong today. Sitting in the turquoise leather bucket seat he turned the key and revved the engine. At this point things inexplicably started to go wrong.

Sirens wailed their annoying noise two notches above deafening and two bicycles screeched to a halt next to the revving Mustang.

Dantalion turned to discover what all the commotion was about. "Is this your car sir?" enquired an irritatingly keen, retired policeman, who dismounted his ride (not forgetting to rest his push bike on a 'look at me, I'm so uncool stand') and finger by finger loosened his black leather gloves before removing them.

"Yeah, what of it? Turn those bloody sirens off!" Dantalion saw no reason to respect humans who he considered to be an inferior beast to a demon.

The second gentlemen now dismounted his bicycle and approached Dantalion. Not a retired policeman this time, more a frustrated bouncer who'd failed the police academic tests while alive. Dantalion sensing that violence was fast approaching chuckled to himself. A feeble human was no match for a demon no matter how large the human was.

Exuding self-confidence, the first human proceeded with his interrogation. "Is this a combustible engine that you have fired up, sir?"

"Yes. What of it?" he repeated with contempt.

"Then I am arresting you for contravening article 4b sub-section 2 of the unofficial laws of heaven." Addressing the bouncer he continued: "Withhold the criminal and impound his car."

Keeping direct eye contact with both officers, Dantalion slowly and with menacing purpose got out of his car. This was the moment his day really started to nose dive. Fists tingling in anticipation of a fight he moved forward. He always found humans' rules of fighting strange. Mistake one, they have rules, which in a fight really restricts your chance of winning. (He had seen humans fight and they always waited for each other to be ready.) Mistake two, why wait? Hit them on the head before they stand a chance. Arms raised in the air ready to bosh he annoyingly remembered. He remembered a specific instruction direct from the Devil's own mouth. "No violence!" The sentence rang in his head as the bouncer plonked his big fist down on it.

"Oh bugger!"

It took Dantalion all his demonic strength to fight the urge to wallop the human back.

Half an hour later he sat brooding in a cramped trailer being towed back to the 'police station' behind the ex bouncer's push bike. He wasn't constrained by handcuffs or prevented from leaping out by steel bars, but he had promised the devil he'd stay incognito and evading arrest was not the way to go. To make matters worse they kept the damned sirens on the whole way back.

The 'station' was in fact Guy's home. Guy, being the ex bouncer, had been named like all Guys - lazily. Similar to naming a horse, Stallion, or a chicken, Hen, Guy had effectively been named after his sex. His home looked like a police station, smelt like a police station and was in fact not a police station. There is no crime in heaven and no need to police an epidemic crime wave of nothingness. This did nothing to deter Guy. He'd made it to heaven where all his dreams should come true so he was jolly well going to be a policeman whether they liked it or not. For years after landing in heaven Guy patrolled the streets keeping all safe from the horrors of angels and angelic people. A lone crusader in a world without crime. What Guy needed was criminals and the only thing better than someone to arrest was a partner, a fellow officer to patrol with. To Guy's great joy, one glorious morning a year ago a fellow officer of the law moved in next door.

Roger had served in the police force his whole working life but never gained promotion up the great ladder of a policeman's potential career. An impressive achievement considering the time he had worked there. Roger was much more concerned with minor details than catching murderers. He was a prolific arrester. Never promoted but constantly moved by his superior officers who (and Roger could never understand why) found him irritatingly annoying. He'd been moved around so often that he would find himself transferred back to departments he'd worked in before.

Roger promptly joined the police force when he entered heaven. It now consisted of two 'officers'. He made sweeping changes to the uniform and rewrote many of the laws. Laws that possessed no legal status but ones that they nevertheless upheld. Guy,while alone, mainly patrolled looking for master criminals, murderers, granny muggers and other such horrors. Never once finding one he had actually zero arrests to his name. Floored from the start, he held no hope of ever arresting a soul due to Saint Peter stubbornly, and Guy would say selfishly, refusing to let these monsters in.

This all changed with Roger. The first arrest they made together involved a pedestrian. She was unaware of her 'criminal' act and was surprised to find herself being interviewed for walking on the 'wrong side' of the path. Apparently, so she was informed, walking on the left hand side was only permitted after midday. This type of 'policing' for minor 'offences' kept happening. Their mantra was 'quantity over quality'. Guy felt a rush of excitement at every arrest but the buzz would never last for long. Minor crimes were not what he'd signed up for. But arresting this Dan, as he called himself, was a major coup. A crime of such stature that it was in fact a real, recognised crime and not a made up offence like the others.

Leading Dan into the interrogation room they sat him down, Guy secretly wishing he was allowed to handcuff him for dramatic effect. Roger with clipboard paper and pen at the ready started the interrogation.

"Full Name?"

"Dantalion."

Guy was already fed up with this wishy washy technique. Standing up abruptly, causing his chair to slide back and crash into the wall, he slammed both hands down on the table, leaned forward and repeated the question in more certain terms. "He said name you low life criminal. Not just your first name we want your full name. Don't even think about using a fake name, we have ways of finding out if you are telling the truth."

"I told you, Dantalion," he replied leaning forward to match Guy's stare. Remembering the Devil's instructions he quickly sat back down in his chair, took on a manner of calmness and added in the most polite way: "Us demons do not use surnames. I believe from what I have read a surname is something to do with what you humans call family. We demons do not have an equivalent of family so have no need of a surname. "

Roger, wanting to keep the conversation calm took command again ushering Guy to sit back down.

"Right. We shall put your name as Dantalion Dantalion as both parts are required for the form. Age? That is, age at death on earth."

"I told you - I am a demon. So I did not die on earth. I have no age." As long as the form was filled out Roger would be satisfied. Having correct information was a secondary consideration.

"Ok I will put 50 for now until we find your birth certificate."

"Officers, is this all necessary? I have accidentally through forgetfulness started my car. I put my hands up and apologise profusely. Can I not just promise to never do this again and be off? I am in rather a rush you see. If there is anything you require I am sure I can help." A smile crossed the demon's face.

Guy almost exploded through excitement. Not only did they have this man on engine related charges but here he was openly trying to bribe two officers of the law. Rising again with explosive force and using his best 'angry policeman' voice, he said: "You dare try to bribe us. Do you know what the punishment for this is?!"

"No tell me officer what is it?" Dantalion was at the point of getting annoyed but still just keeping it under control. He knew his time on the beaches was being limited by these revolting humans.

"It is.. It's ummm. Roger, tell this criminal what the punishment is for attempted bribery."

Flicking through the rule book so carefully constructed by Roger, he came to an alarming conclusion. There was no mention of bribery. It was never a crime he had dealt with on earth so Roger failed to include it in heaven. If one took a glance through the book they might notice other glaring omissions like robbery or arson.

Whispering in Guy's ear he admitted that they actually had no legal right to add the charge of bribery to Dantalion's crimes.

"OK Dan, for now we will ignore your attempted bribe." Guy was put out at having to drop this charge, so sat back down in a huff.

"Now, returning to the form. What is your creed? Angel or human?"

Not so much snapping but more going into the first stages of annoyance Dantalion shouted back: "I'm not a fucking human or Angel. I've told you twice already - I'm a demon!"

At this point it dawned on Dantalion that he had now admitted to being a demon three times. He was pretty sure one thing the devil did not want him to do was admit to being a demon on this undercover task.

It was also at this point that Roger and Guy finally acknowledged that they had arrested a demon. Panic ran across their faces as they struggled to work out what to do. Guy took control and went for it, all guns blazing. "We've got you now, Sunny Jim. No more demonly crimes for you. You'll be lucky to ever be let out again once you're banged up in jail. We are hereby formally charging you for being a demon, server of the devil, keeper of hell.."

"Er, Guy."

"Spy of the underworld.."

"Guy."

Irritated in his moment of glory by being interrupted, Guy huffed back: "What is it Roger?!"

"I'm sorry about this but," Roger paused in embarrassment "but being a demon is not actually a crime." Roger had again been thumbing through the law book and inexplicably there was no mention of demons. "We can still charge him for breaking the combustible engine laws though," hoping to cheer Guy up a little.

Dantalion watched bemused by these idiotic humans. Working it over in his head he realised that his cover was now blown so there was not much need to be subtle round these two imbeciles any longer. With Guy and Roger in a state of consternation the demon drew himself up to full height, took hold of the table with one hand and smashed it against the ceiling. "I charge you two dimwits with being human scum."

"You can't do that," Roger protested with the words sounding like they were not too sure themselves.

Guy went for a more aggressive protest. Lunging at Dantalion he got as far as the now missing table before being pinned to the floor effortlessly by the demon. "Now gentlemen, you two are going to sit in this room until tomorrow. No attempting to escape or shouting for help. I think you will agree I am letting you off lightly. Other less sophisticated demons than myself would rip your heads off just for fun but I know I can trust you to stay in here. Can't I?"

Roger nodded and Guy muffled a sound to confirm. "Excellent, then I must depart. I have beaches to visit and people to see."

Leaving the station Dantalion 'borrowed' a police bike and headed for a bar. Before entering heaven he'd been informed Zed was drinking there and with the bike it wouldn't take too long to find.

"Oh fuck."

Well if Dantalion knew how to ride a bike it wouldn't. Tangled up in the bike he struggled to free himself. Cursing he untangled himself and threw it off. One characteristic that all Demons possess is strength. Dantalion, becoming angered, had flung the bike with all his might and now standing, up and dusting himself off he was blissfully unaware of the impending impact his head was about to receive from the bike's return to ground level.

"Arghh!"

Again, entangled with the bike he wrestled with the steel frame until free once more. Covered in mud and his clothes soaked in a puddle, he sat staring at the now bent bike. His face drooped and with all energy zapped, he gave a sigh. The boss won't like it but he was going to abort the mission. The policemen had held him up for so long that there was no telling where Zed could be now and anyway he was not trailing round heaven covered in mud. It hadn't been a good day: he hadn't found Zed, he hadn't been to the beach or savoured an ice cream and he hadn't driven his prized Mustang. It was time to go home and face the music.

Chapter Fourteen

Looking bedraggled and feeling very much like an injured tortoise half way through racing an aggressively competitive hare, Zed urgently needed some mental cheerleading. The assumption Zed had made that heaven would have pubs every stone's throw or so apart was proving imprecise. His body now felt that the balance between walking and pub pit stops was running dangerously close to Zed's physical limit.

He took inspiration from the greats: Jesus overcoming fasting in the desert, Buddha meditating for days on end. He drew courage and strength from heroes of years past yet he was still close to giving up. Sweating, out of breath, starving and gagging for a cold beer he imagined not many in heaven's history had gone through such pain. It had been a whole two hours of solid walking maybe even two hours five minutes - admittedly with regular sit down breaks so not altogether 'solid' in the conventional sense.

Coming out of the pub, he'd followed a cobbled path through what seemed to be a high street of shops. It looked like a normal town but on closer examination you could see the differences. Everything had a shine or sheen. It was hard to explain but things sort of shimmered in heaven. He also noticed the sky again was cloud free, perhaps even weather free, it seemed intent on showing off its perfect blue complexion. "Do weather and seasons exist in heaven?" he pondered. Did he need a woolly hat and jacket for this journey? Or maybe the opposite and shorts, sunglasses and sun cream are required. "That's it!" he realised what was missing from the sky. Although cloud free, there was no sun. Scanning the sky to double check, he confirmed the sky was definitely minus its friend the sun. Then how was there light and why was there night? After a moments thought he concluded there was no point wasting his limited brainpower;

he would add this to his list of his many unanswered questions.

Topping his list-that-would-never-be-answered questions - the one that bugged him most concerned his fellow souls. Since popping into heaven, there were always plenty of people milling around, all looking pretty happy. Now he noticed yet another heaven exclusive feature - everyone spoke English. Some with foreign accents but all spoke in English.

Zed took decisive action and out of character asked a passing stranger. "Excuse me, but I was just wondering why you were speaking the Queen's tongue yet you sound dreadfully German?"

Carefully he had chosen the least weird looking human he could find just in case they tried to extend this brief chat.

"You don't know?"

"I know not what not to know about."

"What you on about? Do you know or not? Speak English man."

"Sorry, I meant I don't know."

"In heaven we all hear the same language. So when you speak to me it sounds German."

"Amazing. This God chappy has it all sorted. Ever met the fella?"

"Nope, no one has. Some people still think he doesn't exist - like heaven isn't proof enough!"

"Some people will believe what they are told yet others will always believe what's not there," Zed said. "Nice chatting, hope to meet again."

Reverting back to his normal, antisocial character, Zed decided to leave quickly in case the German went all preachy on him. He set off with a bit more bounce in his step, having answered one of many questions. An impressive achievement he thought.

It took Zed a good few hours to walk through the shopping area. He learnt a lot talking to people. Some conversations were invited, others offered anyway. He found out that everyone is given a house in heaven; that every Christmas is a white Christmas; and there really is a Santa. Days last for twenty-seven hours and no one knows why. If you want to get picky, and many geeks do, a day cannot be measured in hours, as time does not exist in heaven. People do not age and heaven has no equivalent fear of the universe ending. Time is faked so plants will grow and night and day exist but it's not a dimension as on earth. When Einstein first heard the notion of timeless time in heaven he went into such a strop and demanded to be sent to hell. He's calmed down now; time is a great healer - or it would be if time existed.

He had asked everyone about crossing the borders of heaven but no one seemed to have the urge to try. One older woman said her husband left to explore heaven but never come back. After listening to her moans, Zed understood why her dear husband went MIA. The only person he was sure would have crossed borders was the map man; it hadn't occurred to him at the time to ask.

If time could be reversed, which we now all know it cannot (for reversing something that doesn't exist is contrary to reason), many a question would be asked. 'Do I need a passport for starters?'

The streets were less busy now as he entered a road with housing estate-esque features, but not like ones you would recognise. Every house was different. Most had big gardens; there were cottages with thatched roofs, ultra modern cubes, Edwardian style red brick town houses and the odd small, unimaginatively designed home. None seemed to be the same and most were hideously grand and needlessly large.

Stopping in his tracks, or more accurately slowing from almost motionless walking speed to fully motionless, Zed felt an icy chill down his spine. He could sense a stalking stare watching his every move. Slowly turning round he was happy to see an ear-to-ear smile instead of foaming fangs.

"Hey Zed," said a man with a Texan accent sporting an orange tan.

"Howdy."

"The name's Johnson. I'm the building agent for your new house. Let's go into my office and talk."

Throwing his arm around Zed he ushered him towards this so-called office.

Feeling he should protest at being led away, Zed did his best and asked a polite question. "You're my what? And how'd you know my name?"

"Building agent. You're on my list. Look here." And sure enough there he was - name and photo. "Did they not explain at the gate? I swear they are getting slack there. One of the many perks here in heaven is you get to design your own dream house. My job's to take down your design and then, voila, it will be built. Never know how it gets built so quick but best not ask questions eh? I mean, did the great Pharaohs worry about how their pyramids got built? Did they care that thousands of slaves would die? Hell no, so why should I?"

"There are slaves in heaven?"

"No, you arse, it was just a figure of speech."

"That's a relief. But for me there's no need for a dwelling to be built. I'm not staying."

"What ya talking crap for. Course you're staying, where else you gonna go? Hell?"

"No I explained it badly. I'm not staying in this time zone of heaven. I plan to cross the border and find my parents."

"Your parents not in this zone? How unlucky mate. Guess I never thought that some people would be in that situation.

Anyways, course there's a need. I'll get a talking to if we don't build your house so don't let old Johnson down."

Zed being a nice man quickly agreed to get it done then planned to make a sharp exit so he could resume his journey swiftly.

Meanwhile, very nearby, Harold was coming to terms with his predicament. Being tied up in his own office cupboard had never been mentioned in any of the many training videos enforced on him over the years. He knew how to lift heavy items correctly, position his chair at the perfect height and recite all the fire regulations, but escaping from a cupboard while tied up had been vastly overlooked.

One minute a nice man was asking about moving his house from the Middle Ages to this plot and the next he was on the floor being held down by four pesky animals of unknown species, gagged and tied up. Maybe it was a prank but April the first was not for another month.

"Right Zed this is your plot. You can have and do whatever you want to this land. What house did you dream of owning or building back down on earth?"

Giving this some serious consideration Zed realised he had no clue what sort of house he should ask for. Never had he wasted time on earth thinking about his dream home. It just never occurred to him that a full detailed plan should be made before death along with your will. "Well I always liked my next door neighbour's house. I'd look at mine and think 'I wish I could move next door'."

"Great, let's build that. How was it different to yours? Describe it Zed and we will build the house of your dreams!"

"Oh jeez, how do I describe my home?" he thought. Zed would struggle to describe a blank piece of paper let alone a three dimensional inhabitable dwelling. "The house was the same as mine but cleaner and newer looking; oh and a small conservatory extension on the rear."

Johnson was taken aback. Being American, when describing anything attached to dreams, the adjective big or large or massive would be heavily used. "Let's get this straight. You can have the house of your dreams and you chose to have your old crappy house but cleaned and a conservatory stuck on the back?"

"When you put it like that perhaps I should ask for more."

Sensing Zed could do with some decisive decision-making help he volunteered. "Do you want a swimming pool, tennis court, a bar?"

Without a moment's hesitation, Zed answered (while doing a jig of unknown origins in child-like elation). "A bar, a bar, I'd love a bar."

The possibility of living in a house with a bar was close to Zed's peak excitement. Knowing he could have a bar brought what Buddhists would call enlightenment to Zed's spirit, or soul or whatever he was now - who cares as long as he could have a bar.

"You shall have your bar and a clean house. Now internal decorations are done later so we just need you to sign here, and here, and your house will be built. Yer sure you don't want to super size the house?"

The pen was grabbed and signed speedier than the reigning hundred-metre light wave champion. And just like that the house appeared. Now magic doesn't exist in heaven but some phenomena occur that boggle the mind and prove tricky to explain without the term magic. General consensus on these 'magical' events is 'Why does something happen? Well it just does, so accept it'.

"Come on in," Johnson said leading the way through his new house. "This is your house. Isn't it perfect?"

To be frank Zed wasn't impressed. Turns out, his description of the perfect house was somewhat on the shoddy side. Seeing his house before him - but cleaner - lost its appeal within ten seconds. His imagination had let him down, but his brain came to the rescue shouting, 'get to the bar you dim wit!'.

"Er, could we possibly see the bar?"

"Anything for you Zed. This way."

Inside the walls were plain and there was no furniture. 'Guess this gets sorted later,' he thought. Through the bland hallway and out into the featureless garden they walked and there, at the bottom of the garden, was his bar. At first glance the term 'bar' could be replaced by 'over sized wooden shed loitering with intent to be a bar'. However, knowing what should be inside his 'shed of dreams' allowed Zed to look past its brown featureless frame; for to Zed's eyes, it appeared as a bar of glorious beauty, illuminated by a light beam shining through a halo sprouting from the roof. Almost knocking Johnson over, Zed galloped for the first time in years. He reached out to touch his bar and felt the rough unsanded outside door, painted in shed brown; he whispered sweet nothings to it before throwing the door open to reveal the glory within. A huge slab of polished dark walnut stretched from one side to the other. Five pumps teasingly suggested that cold beer could be imminently available and along the rear wall Victorian glass cabinets overflowed with spirits, wines and glasses.

"I'm guessing, Zed, you'll be happy here won't you? It will take a while to sort out so probably best for you to hang around a while and scrap any crazy travelling plans of yours."

The headlights from the bar turned off in Zed's rabbit eyes and he remembered: "Of course I won't need any of this; I am off to find my parents. But what happens if they don't have a bar? This is a rather nice place."

"I could stay here for a while before I'm up and off to find them," he agonised.

Zed's brain was struggling as this argument played out in his head, and things were not helped when a very angry, half tied-up man, and the Angel Elemiah from the hotel, stormed in.

Without any greetings, the Angel started chanting while the angry man shouted every swear word Zed knew and a few that were extinct by the time Zed was born.

"Excuse me, who are you?" Zed politely asked the now ready-to-explode, angry home intruder.

The furious man briefly stopped shouting while making theatrical gestures with his arms and turned to Zed. He had a head-exploding colour of bright red and was, in Zed's opinion, risking a heart attack.

Speaking in a contrastingly calm voice the man spoke. "Oh hello Zed. I am your house builder, Harold."

Chapter Fifteen

There are Angels who posses great strength; Angels that can sing with such soothing beauty the mere sound can heal a dying man; ones who have knowledge beyond any human achievement; and ones that offer divine advice but never for free.

Earlier in the day, (before Zed had commissioned his house), Elemiah was in need of some advice about Zed but had no intention of consulting an Angel. Unlike most Angels she enjoyed the company of humans. They were not as arrogant. Through her hotel business she spent most of her time talking to or studying the human race. She, like God, could see their beauty when others just saw wild, ungrateful animals.

But she was not on her way to a human either. Although fun to talk to, they were not the cleverest and their best advice normally involved praying or some other pointless activity. It was a cat she wanted to consult with - a big, furry, fat cat.

Arriving at the cat's house, an everyday terrace sort of house, she rang the bell.

"Enter," shouted someone from within.

"Just let me in would you," Elemiah grunted a not so polite a response.

"You know the rules."

"But I'm an Angel not a human," she protested.

"You all look the same to me. If you want to come in then you will use the human entrance." Although Elemiah had no way of seeing, she knew this was said with a huge grin.

She thought about arguing but also knew no good would come of it, so gave in. Bending down onto all fours, quickly checking no other Angels were watching, she rammed her head at the door, opening a flap just about large enough for your average human to squeeze through - with a good deal of effort. Elemiah pulled herself through the human flap and with one extra hard last push to force her wings through, she found herself flat on her face with only a cold concrete floor to rest on. A wet sand paper lick did nothing to brighten her mood.

"Come on, up you get. I've got some hot milk waiting for you."

Patches the cat did not like his name; he was in fact called Rufus, King Rufus the Great, if you were to use his full name. Always insulted that his human feeders dared to call him 'Patches' when he was so self-conscious of his patchy fur. He didn't go around calling the fat, ugly one 'Sweat Patch' did he? Even though Sweat Patch would feed him mashed up beef coloured chicken in a tiny, dirty bowel while Sweat Patch ate sweet smelling salmon torturously close by. Now in heaven and no longer reliant upon humans to feed him, Patches decided it was time he chose his own name. King Rufus the Great he thought rolled of the tongue perfectly. No one else agreed.

A warm cup of milk while stretched out on a soft rug, next to a roaring fire, eased Elemiah's anger with Rufus.

"So you're saying this human is special?" Rufus spat the word human out with detest and rolled his green round eyes.

"Yes. Even though there seems nothing special about him, I have this feeling.."

"Yeah right, a drunk feeling perhaps?"

"Quiet and let me explain about Zed. And anyway, that was only one time and he almost did turn out to be Satan's son."

Holding back laughter, Rufus purred in delight. "The other Angels, they still laugh at you?"

"That's it, I'm off. I came here for help and instead you give me abuse."

"Lighten up Elemiah! Ok, I'm all ears. What feeling did you have which had no alcohol related influences?"

Giving a moment's thought on whether she'd made a mistake coming here, Elemiah relaxed and sat back down. "It's as though I can see an aura of light around him. Not with my eyes but with my mind. A warning light perhaps - illuminating Zed, alerting me to him. I would have dismissed it as nothing but I've something telling me in a way I can't describe - I have a responsibility and the light is there to guide me." Rufus, who wanted to make a number of jokes, knew when to be serious and lay stretched out by the fire in deep cat thought. "Us cats can sense things our human overlords knew nothing about in their pointless lifetime. They knew nothing about the voices in the wind or the life of the shadows, but you Angels do seem to have senses beyond the humanoids." He paused and purred a dramatic purr. "A cat much wiser than me once told a story."

"No Rufus, not a bloody story. It will be about mice again."

"You offend me. This story has no mice."

"OK, hurry up then; let me hear the wise old cat's story."

"Who said the cat was old? You must learn to listen to what is said not what your head thinks is said. One night a highly skilled hunter of a cat was out stalking her prey. She had followed the big juicy mou... rat, I said rat, for enough time now and was about to pounce. Moving her weight to her rear paws, legs bent to get maximum spring from her deadly jump she hesitated. The rat was staring right at her. Dark small eyes locked, not blinking. This wasn't right - rats don't stare, if they see you they run. A feeling of danger rushed through her hypersensitive senses. Everything screamed at her to stop, turn around and find a different mouse (bugger, rat) to eat that night. But the sweet juicy smell of the rat was too much. She leapt forward front paws stretched out; her razor sharp claws shot out. And then she woke up. She woke up in heaven."

Not particularly gripped by the story Elemiah was startled into listening mode at hearing the cat had died.

"The details of how she met her death are so grotesquely awful I am never allowed to describe them."

"Hold on Rufus. Are you trying to tell me I'm going to die a horrific death?"

Allowing a laugh Rufus reassured her. "No you silly Angel, I'm just saying the cat ignored what was shouting at her, screaming at her to pay attention. It would be wise not to ignore what's shouting at you. Go and follow Zed. Observe him, see what's so special and most importantly. . . "

"Yes go on what must I do?"

"Go and fetch me some more warm milk."

Chapter Sixteen

There are many debates, mainly accompanied by an alcoholic beverage, over who should be granted the eternal gift of heaven. Of course, some by default fall to eternal damnation: murderers, dictators, terrorists, koala bears to list just a few. One type of human is mentioned more often than not in such debates and mostly put into the camp of 'keep them out of heaven'. Yet wandering around heaven you will bump into them and find that today, in heaven, they are just as annoying as back on earth - the 'not so lesser-spotted salesmen'. Should a person who, in their words, 'enhances the truth to provide essential services to the human race' and in everyone else's words 'lies aggressively with one goal to take your money at whatever cost', be allowed into heaven? The problem with putting a blanket ban on these people is many have the irritating ability to blag better than Saint Blagger, the Blagsmith from Blagtown. They could convince Eskimos to purchase air conditioning for their igloos and sell water to a well with six months' free flood insurance. Saint Peter, over the years, feeling fed up, always losing what seemed perfectly logical arguments to these lie weavers, now let them straight in. "It's just not worth the effort," he remarked upon being questioned about his lax attitude and who, apart from salesmen, dares to argue with Saint Peter?

Zed, perplexed by his current predicament of playing host to two arguing men and the delightful Elemiah resolved the mystery.

"Ah I see," thought Zed, "he's angry as the other guy got to me first. It must be two overly competitive salesmen, no doubt in competition with each other to get the salesman of the month award. The first guy must have stolen his sell in an unsportsman like way and lost this second chap a large bonus. A bonus of what I don't know as everything here is free."

Zed's attention now turned to the American who was frantically shouting at him.

"You must stay here. Your wishes will all come true here. Do not travel out of this zone as only danger awaits."

"Salesmen," thought Zed, "they will tell you anything for a sell."

"Everyone calm down please. I'm sure we can arrange something to help both your sales' figures." Feeling like he understood their anger, Zed wanted to lower the noise level and stop the arguing. He detested arguing. Essentially, arguing is a noise of high decibels that resolves nothing, causes stress and can lead to something worse - violence. If it were possible, Zed would abolish arguing. Do sloths argue? No, and they seem pretty content, if a bit lazy.

The plea by Zed fell on deaf ears; the argument grew louder and more intense. Zed could feel tension cracking in the air. Johnson, as if reaching his peak of feuding, stopped shouting and looked at Zed. The stare intensified passing the limit of reasonable time to stare and crossing over into the awkward 'why are you staring at me' zone. Zed could swear the guy's eyes were pulsating red.

Zed did not imagine this. Indeed the staring eyes were throbbing a colourful stare directly at him. Johnson's eyes were lit up like red plasma. The anger was like a flux rushing through his body, flowing into his hands forcing them to clench tightly and out through his eyes lighting them up with the energy absorbed through the anger flux. What was this Angel doing here interrupting his plan? Unable to control his rage, Johnson thrust his hand towards Zed. A sound, like highly charged static electricity, filled the air and without making physical contact, flung Zed across the room slamming him against the wooden bar wall.

In shock, Zed slumped bent over on the floor wheezing, still attempting to calm the situation but unable to get any words out.

The Angel was chanting manically now and Zed could not answer why. His senses were all over the place. Air around Zed felt, and in a certain light, looked to be sucked towards the American, drawn by an invisible force. The flimsy wooden planks on the shed floor vibrated attempting to escape the nails pinning them down; and all his beautifully lined up bottles along the bar rattled alarmingly and threatened to dance the dance of death onto the floor.

Recovering slightly, Zed asked: "Excuse me, did you build this house with earthquake resistant walls?" That must be what's happening thought Zed – an earthquake in heaven. Each vowel exiting his mouth disappeared into the vortex of air rushing towards Johnson. Not even Zed heard what he'd just asked. He didn't get a reply. Like a whale diving belly first onto a bouncy castle, the floor seemed to jump ten feet up, and that was enough for Zed. He knew how to protect himself - duck and cover. But there was no bloody furniture; so no table to duck under. Damn this house. Going for the lesser known, or taught 'earthquake protection technique' he lay on the floor, curled up into a hedgehog ball, with his hands trying to protect his fragile head, and prayed.

What he missed, as seeing with your eyes closed is impossible even in heaven, was the floor cracking and slowly ripping open under the American. Anyone unlucky enough to peer into the crack would see boiling lava spraying up from below, moving around as though possessed; lava that seemed to be reaching out searching for something to feel its skin-melting heat.

Screaming in rage, Johnson's appearance changed for the worse. Horns were sucked out of his head, his skin turned green and the demon Xaphan showed his true form. Most observers would have placed a large bet that at this intense moment there would be no more friendly chatting. They would also lose a lot of money. The Angel suddenly stopped chanting and started to have a quick chat with the demon. Being a fallen Angel, Xaphan and Elemiah knew each other from days gone past. They actually used to get along like a house on fire but things changed when Xaphan attempted to set heaven on fire for a prank. They had a friendly 'long time no see, how's it down there? I know what's going on, the Devil won't get away with it, general everyday sort of chat'.

"We must meet up again one day when you've repented all your sins. But for now I must say bye." And with a wave Elemiah stamped her foot. The noise of an overweight, bloated pig being sucked down a muddy toilet elegantly describes the sound of the demon returning to hell. A rush of air followed him down and the hole slammed shut, leaving no sign it had ever existed.

Bravery comes to many naturally but for Zed it never came. After a good ten minutes of silence, Zed uncurled himself and resumed the position of a brave, unflinching man. Everyone had gone. They must have taken their argument back to the office and left me in peace. Next time he saw Johnson he would enquire how often these earthquakes occur.

Pulling a pint from his bar to calm his nerves, he noticed a golden ticket. Picking it up, squinting to see what it said, for the eyes were still attempting to recover fully from shock, he focused and read:

'One free pass - donkey train to ancient Egypt. No train is faster. No journey more luxurious.'

With his eyes close to recovering, he saw the ticket was nearer to brown not gold.

"Luck is holding my hand today," he thought. "First my own bar and now a ticket for the place I need to go. Coincidence or what?" But then again, this was the bar of his dreams; only a madman or a muppet would walk away from a dream. "I'll sleep on it and have a nightcap or four first." Throwing the ticket down nonchalantly, he poured a drink and made plans to take a well-deserved rest.

Chapter Seventeen

Through millennia of story telling, myths and Chinese whispers, the Devil had grown a bad reputation. 'Bad' being the sort of 'bad' when a honey badger finds you naked in his bed after it explained to yet another ignorant tourist that he was not in fact a badger.

In truth, all rumours told of the Devil – and this is for the benefit of any sinner still alive (to give them a chance to repent) - are watered down compared to the reality in the great pit of hell. Just reading or hearing the facts about the monstrosity of repulsive terror the Devil has inflicted on the damned over millennia would cause such excruciating pain that a bath in volcanic lava would seem like a luxury, all-inclusive holiday.

But in the last hundred years Satan had chilled out. Some blame old age, others thought boredom, his character had definitely mellowed - still despicably evil, but evil with a cherry on top. He now wandered round hell, dishing out punishments with a smile on his face, content with life.

Yet lately the Devil was getting stressed and this Zed business was trying his patience. His weekly torturing routine had intensified; he was losing his temper over the slightest thing. Just the other day someone merely complimented him about his newly purchased brown Oxford style shoes; an unfortunate mistake, as he had neglected to notice they were in fact brown 'cap toe' Oxford shoes not just regular Oxfords. This luckless sycophant, after his calamitous error, found himself having soles of shoes nailed to his feet each day. The Devil's always keen to make the punishment fit the crime.

Currently the Devil held in one vast skull-crushing hand, suggestively motioning in a menacingly evil way, an oversized pineapple coated with bullet ants and a petrified new hell dweller in the other hand. This would have sent shivers of excitement down his spine in the good old days but today his heart was elsewhere. Apologising profusely, the torture session was brought to a premature end and he wandered off deep in thought to his personal chamber.

He always felt at home here, despite still living in exile. The walls and ceiling were blood red. The decor was gothic and reminiscent of many a church. Sitting down in his great golden jewel encrusted throne he pondered events so far. He was disappointed in Dantalion. Xaphan had done everything perfectly. It was that pesky Angel interfering that buggered up his plan more painfully than a pineapple. Keeping him in that house would have made it easy. The Angel must have suspected something. "For fuck sake!" he roared in a way only the Devil could.

Knowing that Zed was the key to having everything he'd ever wanted annoyed him. If this pawn had been someone impressive then OK. But Zed was a meagre unimportant nobody. A nothing. Yet he had eluded two of his most trusted and dangerous demons. What the fuck was going on.

Then he sat back and grinned.

Chapter Eighteen

Waking up with a hangover inflicted on yourself at your own bar is unlike any normal hangover experience. It's a great feeling. The dry mouth is replaced by drooling lips; they know your next pint is just a few steps away. The banging head turns into a rhythmic tune dancing you towards your bar. Or at least Zed imagined it would be. Turns out, waking up on the cold, rough, wooden floor of your new house, with no furniture, (which directly implies no soft comfy bed), sucks. 'Ooohhhhh,' said his head. 'Owwwww,' exclaimed his body; his internal organs thanked him sarcastically for reducing their life expectancy yet again. His brain, being well rehearsed, fired flares around Zed's body lifting him up from his zombified state, dragging his legs as he walked and stretching out his arms to take the impact of any collision. The brain knew a shower could at least kick start sleeping senses and get the body motoring again.

"Arghhhh Christ!"

Zed produced the universally recognised reaction to an unexpectedly ice cold shower. "What am I doing?" he thought with the first signs of life returning to his body. "No furniture, no hot water and a God forsaken hangover." This dream house, in supersonic quick time had manifested into a house of nightmares.

Drenched, freezing cold and miserable, not much could get worse. He was now at the bottom of any low point ready to climb back to happiness. What could possibly dig the pit of despair any deeper you may ask? No towels – now that would do the trick. Fossilised fish fingers were the words that came to mind - there was nothing to dry his body with. Bedraggled and fed up Zed knew of only one way; he shook his weary body like a shaggy dog and sat sulking outside by his bar, stark naked, drying in the sun. Although in heaven there was no sun - just heat from 'somewhere'.

At least this gave him time for contemplation. He could renovate this house; he could make a few friends and have them round occasionally for refreshments and aperitifs. There was possibly a private club he could join and, as everything is free, without the expensive fees. A character reference presumably would be required to keep the riff raff out but Zed assumed he'd fly through the tests.

Slowly his brain realised he was thumbing something in his hand. How this thing materialised there he had no idea and CCTV footage along with forensic analysis would provide little clues. He could have sworn it just appeared. It was the ticket from yesterday. He'd forgotten all about it after his fifth nightcap and given it no more thought since.

Turning the brown ticket over he read the details. It was for a donkey train run by the Francesco brothers. "Since time began," it claimed. Strange name for a train but hey, if you can call a car a Jaguar, then why not a train a Donkey. A time and date were printed in bold font:

12:33 Today.

Firstly, how did the ticket know it's today and secondly, if this train was like ones he was used to, there was no need for such a precise time.

Instantaneous decisions were not Zed's forte but breaking a rule of a lifetime, he made one. "Well what the hell," he thought, 'It would be nice to see the old fellas again and such a waste not to use this free ticket." With a glancing look at his bar (so as to not get too emotional) he upped and left his house - just like that.

"Arghhh!" screamed the now mentally scarred old woman who watched Zed exiting his house.

Returning instantly back inside, he remembered his clothes and set off for a second time. Now that the neighbours thought Zed was either a flasher or nudist, it was best he'd decided not to stay.

Before departing a second time, the thought occurred to Zed: his sense of direction matched his ability to design houses. For anyone who's forgotten and needs a small reminder, his designing skills were below par - some ten miles below par. A scientist once described luck as the assistance of unknown quandaries providing an unexpected but pleasant result. Some people seem to have more luck than others; actually every person is born filled with the same amount of luck. Some get great bursts of luck - perhaps a hole in one or winning the lottery - while others leak luck constantly in such small amounts they don't even notice. Zed expelled a medium dose of luck and checked his ticket once again. On the back were some directions and an address for the train station, or more precisely a detailed description of the route to take.

Turn right out of your house. Carry on until you see the old woman who says 'Hi'. Turn left, walk past several Morris dancers. When you hear a French sounding argument, turn right and carry on until you see the great tent.

"Well I never, Morris dancers make it to heaven!" His surprise at Morris dancers prancing round heaven, summed up Zed's blind acceptance of life. He picked up on the Morris point yet the amazingly personalised, future-predicting ticket made no impact on Zed's thoughts. To him they were just directions to be followed.

Of course, predicting the future is impossible. Yet in heaven things that are impossible seem to happen even though they are impossible. God could explain how this happens but it's impossibly complex and hence impossible to understand.

Not questioning the accuracy of a free ticket, he turned right and headed off in search of the woman. Indeed ten minutes later with hopes fading, a nice South African sounding woman tending to her red roses said 'Hi!'.

Turn left thought the brain and it then took another thirty seconds to remind Zed's mouth to say hi back.

"How rude," the woman said. "How did that awful man get into heaven? Peter's really dropped his standards lately. He shouldn't be letting any riff raff in."

Hands in his pockets, Zed hummed a melody, happy for the first time that day. A poor start can be turned swiftly around when things go your way. With the first direction marker passed as predicted, it should bode well for the rest of the journey. Stopping to admire a chocolate box house with picturesque gardens, his day was swiftly ruined.

There are occasions where one's brain chooses to ignore certain chunks of information, quarantining them until nearer the time when they're needed. The next point of interest mentioned was Morris dancers. On first reading this in his house, Zed was wary at the prospect of fending off overly happy, eager Morris men. Now approaching the time he'd walk through this dangerous species, he went from happy to forlorn.

"Oh bother, next on route are the Morris dancers." He knew he was getting close to their habitat as bunting dangled threateningly on every house and lamppost, stretching across each road. Some animals wee to mark their territory; Morris men notify others of their territory with bunting. The more powerful the group residing in the area, the tackier and longer the bunting will be.

There's a reason bunting only comes out occasionally - because it's horrendously tacky. To find a lesser-spotted Morris man, you first find the bunting and then listen for the dreaded sound, and sure enough, getting louder as Zed approached the Morris epicentre, he heard the jingle of bells.

Posters advertising 'Heaven's Largest Village Fete' were dotted everywhere, nailed to trees. Zed hated village fetes. The opposite can be said of a Morris dancer; to them, fetes are heaven. Unlike everywhere else in the known universe, they are always welcomed and watched at village fetes. Occasionally, they even get a round of applause - and not just out of sympathy. Legend has it that the bravest of the Morris men ventured into town centres to display the excitement and skills of Morris dancing. The town folk ridiculed and humiliated the brave Morris dancers and from that day they've sworn revenge. A Morris dancer called Gary, went by himself a second time, confident he would be cheered and hero-worshipped. Since that day, he's not spoken a word and cowers in the corner of his local pub, drinking the days away, trembling at the sound of a bell or Morris cheer.

"Right, how shall I deal with this predicament?" Hearing the sound of dancing Morrisers, Zed was forced into devising a cunning plan. The normal tactics of head down, ignore everything, seldom worked on these people. No, he needed to show interest, get them talking amongst themselves and then slither off when distracted, without them noticing. The plan was tremendous; Zed patted himself on his back.

A few minutes later he was in the battlefield. Entering the lion's den, Zed spotted several groups of Morris men. Staring, he made eye contact with the largest group. Some would say this was a dangerous tactic. The returned smiles sent shivers down his spine, but he knew he would have to stay strong. The dancers wore white traditional Morris clothes, a brown straw hat decorated with multi coloured bands; their arms and legs were wrapped around with bells. Every movement triggered jingles or jangles. To Zed they portrayed the image of pure evil.

"Right they know I'm here, and like a coiled cobra watching a doomed desert rat they will strike soon." This was the epicentre of Morris land.

The lead dancer came forth. "Welcome to Morris Street. The street that is filled with fun all year round." He was smaller and creepier looking than the rest, he had the appearance of a teacher crossed with an evil elf, greasy hair in no particular style and at least six extra bands of evil jingles wrapped around him. His smile reminded Zed that a smile could bring happiness yet can also portray creepiness with greater impact.

"Ah yes fun, I'm sure. The best of fun. I always see you lot at fetes. Will there be a fete here soon?"

"A fete every day is what we aim for. But with all the administration involved and dance practice we can only manage one per fortnight. We were just about to practice. You can watch - it's your lucky day. My name's Robert."

Robert stuck out a hand for Zed to shake with such happy optimism only a Morris man could muster.

"That would be top. Smashing. Go ahead," Zed replied attempting to smile back. The plan was going well. All he needed was to get them dancing and then, kaboom, strike.

The music was folk, the dancing was embarrassing and the jangle of the bells annoying. However Zed noted he seemed to be the only one of this opinion. A large crowd gathered and clapped along. Some children started imitating the Morris men and Zed was convinced he saw a middle aged woman almost faint, like a young teenager meeting their poster idol.

Time was now banging on Zed's brain to hurry up and strike so it could speed up again. For it's not just humans who find time slows down when bored; when it's bored, time itself slows. And time hated going slowly. It especially hated going slowly when everyone raved about the speed of light. It had a secret jealousy that light could go so fast. While time was urging Zed to hurry, he pulled out his metaphorical rabbit and went in for the kill.

"Excuse me," he said, interrupting their main routine, "but I have a question." Robert looked annoyed that someone had dared interrupt the Moriskentanz, the most difficult of all the Morris dances but was also excitedly intrigued as to why anyone would stop for a question. "Yes, what is it you want to know?"

"At a bar the other day someone told me I could never be a Morris dancer as I was not born to be one. Is this true?"

Robert, being born a Morris man, whose father was a Morris man and his father's father and so on was grinning from ear to ear. "Your friend was correct. To be a true Morris man is in your blood." He was about to go into a lengthy lecture on this subject when he was interrupted by a weak, shy voice nearby.

"I wasn't born a Morris man. Does that mean I'm not one?" The Morris men parted to reveal a tall, heavily overweight bloke looking very different to the majority gathered round.

Robert, a bit less confidently, replied: "Well no, you can never be a true Morris man. We let you join in with everything though."

"But last week, when I cleaned the streets for the fete, you said I was a true Morriser?"

"Err, excuse me. But that's not quite correct. In the book of Morris it says you can convert and once able to dance the dance, then thou shall Morris like a true Morris man does. Your thinking is old fashioned, incorrect and offensive." Piped up a young chap forcefully pushing his way through the other Morris men to confront Robert.

Escalating quickly, people were now shouting arguments from all around. Another voice from the crowd bellowed out. And then the once peaceful men of Morris went berserk.

Taking his chance to escape full throttle, he slipped off like a lubed up lioness stalking her prey through the grasses of the Serengeti. Zed made his way through the crowd ready to pounce on his next 'meal', which was the French argument the ticket had foretold. He instinctively knew the argument mentioned on his train ticket would be in this crowd and his ears focused in on a faint sound of 'monsieur'. Two French Morris men were arguing a few meters away. An angry Frenchman is feared world wide, so Zed wisely decided not to interrupt. "No need to slow down here just hang a right and with a good stride I'll be at my destination."

Turning right, he viewed a scene he was not expecting. Initially he went back round the corner to make sure all the houses and angry people were still there. From being in the middle of a built up area with roads, houses, people and other such reassuring signs of civilisation, he suddenly saw stretched out in front of him a desert. Hills of sand framed the horizon with the occasional cartoon inspired image of a cactus. No more people and no path. It was a true desert, golden sands, everlasting horizon and blazing sun - but without the sun as mentioned previously, heaven is lacking in the sun department. The only thing that was not stereotypically desert was an old looking wooden signpost with arrows pointing in several different labelled directions. These included Roman Times, Jurassic, Middle Ages and a slightly smaller one marked 'Donkey Train'.

"Follow that sign," the brain said followed swiftly by the sensible part of the brain piping up. "Sorry to be a nuisance but that desert does not look on the safe side of our normal safe scale we all agreed upon." Zed's brain's response was swift and devastating. "We've given up our bar; nothing will get in our way now. Ok?!"

On he strode with more determination than he had mustered before; large commanding strides to let the desert know who was the boss.

Five exhausting minutes later, he approached the top of the second dune rudely placed between himself and his destination. Gasping for air, craving water and reconsidering this adventure he sat down in a huff. Cursing this stupid decision he'd made so determinedly and spontaneously, the temptation to turn round and give up flowed through Zed's veins.

"Remember the bar. You gave up our dream bar - now get up off your boney behind and walk!" Zed's brain had no sympathy for his tired legs. If they came across a crocodile infested stream the brain would have commanded they go forth, such was its determination.

He continued for an hour or so. Every five or ten minutes the legs would go on strike, and the brain would remind the legs they were not signed up to the workers union so had no legal right to strike, and don't forget - The Bar Sacrifice! Off they would go again until the next leg rebellion. Only after the eighth stop did the brain accept that maybe the legs had a point.

Sitting, with all body parts on strike, Zed slowly became aware of some noise; noise of people; real people; loud people. Mainly people arguing, but real people not the imaginary ones that Zed had made friends with in the sand. Rallying his few ounces of remaining strength, he crawled, grasping at the sand, up the last metre and then wow! What a scene down below! The empty desert was replaced with a hive of activity. Hundreds of people going towards, and streaming out from, what he could only imagine was the Donkey Train station. Where there are people there is water and Zed's mouth was screaming for some. Running, falling and scrambling down the hill, Zed grabbed the first person he saw almost making the poor, old, frail woman collapse. And all he could get out of his bone-dry mouth was a noise that slightly resembled 'water'.

"Get off me young man or I'll scream rape."

"I just want water."

"Rapeeeee!"

"Ok, ok, ok, I'll get off you but please, kind woman, where can I find water?"

"It's next to you, you fecking eejit."

And sure enough, Zed was, much to the amusement of people watching, leaning on a tap clearly marked drinking water.

Diving under the tap, mouth fully open he released the tap. Knowing the near orgasmic feeling that the water would bring, his tongue stuck out wanting the first drops of ice-cold liquid.

"Splghhh owwwww!"

"Oh I am sorry young man I appear to have turned the water to hot. Would you like it turning down ya rapist?"

"You vile serpent of hideous form," is what Zed thought but somehow came out his mouth as "yes please."

He tried again and drank and drank and drank.

After more water than an overly thirsty elephant drinks in a year, he straightened up and surveyed his surroundings. The woman had gone thankfully and had been replaced by Bob, the strange annoying imbecile of a man from the gates.

"Oh gosh, I thought I'd got rid of you. Er, in other words, good to see you again."

"The Lord has yet again made our paths cross. Since I left to do your bidding I've recruited many who now know the name Zed. They have dispersed and each is spreading through the lands the message of your coming. They will not stop, for all must hear of your arrival. Each will walk around heaven until they are back where they started."

This was in fact impossible. On earth it took thousands of years for humans to accept the earth was round. In heaven the Angels are still trying to convince the great human scientists that heaven is flat. The great minds from Earth all ask: "But what is at the edge of heaven?"

"There is no edge of heaven," the Angels reply.

"But that's impossible, if heaven is flat it must have an end," and so go the arguments for hours. But heaven goes on forever and never stops. On earth they say the universe is expanding. But if it is expanding then what was there before the universe expanded into it? If you can answer that, you are half way to understanding how heaven can go on forever.

"Who, what, where are you talking about? Let's go and find a bar so I can work out how to catch my train." Zed was slightly vexed that Bob was here blathering on about a made up fairy tale again.

"Oh master, where are you travelling to?"

"I am off to see my parents hitherto."

"Then alas, we will depart from each other again. But let's drink to our meeting and the future." Bob was now quite the drinker after a lifetime of sobriety.

"What a spot of luck," Zed thought. He'd been furiously calculating an escape plan but no need. Just be patient and humour the guy for an hour or so and then off.

Locating a bar was like finding salt in seawater. The sea of course was, to many an educated Angel, God's greatest error; a humanitarian masterpiece providing earth with a near inexhaustible quantity of drinking water. If only the mix up with sugar and salt could have been prevented. The only positive came from the fishes' unexpected love of salt water.

Just like any port or trading post, the place was littered with bars. They all stretched out along a straight road opposite the donkey train station. The station, as we shall call it, had separate gates for different trains - marked A to G. To be more accurate the 'station' was a humongous tarpaulin held up by scaffolding.

Sitting in the first bar they came to, Zed fumbled his sand filled pocket to locate his ticket. Checking the smaller print the ticket provided further details - Gate E and board when you hear the horn blast thrice.

Zed got up before he'd sat down and ordered two pints of bitter from a lady who possessed skin that only rubbing sand continuously over her face and arms could have produced. He thanked her kindly and carried the two pints back to the table he'd not had time to sit at. This time he bent his knees and made an attempt to settle his bum into the seat for several hours of drinking.

"Baaaaaaaam" went a ridiculously loud horn.

Zed leapt in the air again unable to sit down, making whimpering noises while his eyes looked like a rabbit's caught in headlights. The two luscious looking pints jumped in the air and, although Zed took great care to keep hold of the glasses, the beer had other ideas and leapt out onto his face.

The bar lady cackled a sand-edged sounding laugh. While Bob helped him up and was highly concerned, the overly amused bar woman poured two more and shouted over to them that she would bring the drinks across as he was a danger to others.

Zed thanked her, avoiding eye contact and the extra embarrassment that would cause. Now with both Zed's and Bob's bums firmly planted to their chairs and a beer to celebrate this achievement, Bob started with his questions. He radiated the feeling of a well-shaken bottle of champagne eagerly anticipating the firing of the cork to release the gushing contents in a fountain of glory.

"Tell me everything Zed. I need to know every last detail. Oh, how I wish I had a dictaphone. What have you done so far on your quest? Have you taught, fasted, and performed miracles?"

"I've er, had my house built and then came here via a Morris dance."

"Oh master, you are too modest. How lucky to find some Morris dancers. You know I always suspected I had Morris blood. I'm sure you have mesmerised thousands with your words. Please tell me about your time here and do not play down your experience as doing nothing."

Zed protested like a told off teenager. "But I have. Honest that is all I've done,"

"Preparing your great sermon no doubt. I understand."

Zed's ears were not at 100% which could be attributed to the amount of sand that was making home in them.

"Preparing my great seaman?! What are you rabbiting on about now? Never mind, now go and get another drink before I need to leave."

But it was too late. Thrice went the horns, thrice Zed jumped in shock and thrice did everyone laugh at him.

The two hearty friends embraced, saying their goodbyes wishing for the day they met again to come soon. Well, from Bob's point of view the scene went like that. Zed may tell you that this man Bob attacked him with an uncomfortably long hug that Zed did not reciprocate and departed with a polite goodbye, hoping to never cross paths again.

All seasoned travellers will tell you that on modern transport you can no longer drink the time away waiting for the last call to board. No, you have to get there an hour early and then fight your way for the best seat. Zed, oblivious to these things, rocked up to his gate, smiled, as there was no queue and then made his way to the youngish chap collecting tickets.

"Ticket please."

"Here you go."

A quick stamp and he was let through. Half expecting to be challenged for some sort of identification, the ease of boarding pleased him dearly.

In he went, mildly excited to see the type of train they used in heaven. His bets were for a beautifully crafted steam engine that sped along at an electric pace. What he saw made a loud noise, but not that of an engine. Instead in front of him were about thirty donkeys, all tethered together, and what appeared to be the train driver in traditional Bedouin clothes, and a few others dressed similarly - presumably the cabin crew and the passengers. Not claiming to be an expert in donkeys, Zed knew by just looking that these were the Rolls Royce of donkeys - legs with turbos, fur shaped to be aerodynamically perfect and an eeyore louder than a Harley Davidson.

A donkey stewardess walked past so Zed grabbed her attention. "Pardon me, but I have a ticket and I cannot see a free donkey." Still not seeing the errors in his ways Zed soon learnt that to be late for your train meant awful things were likely to occur.

"The last donkey is just being saddled up, we had a sick one so his replacement has delayed proceedings slightly. He hasn't been out on the train for a few years but I'm sure he'll be fine. The donkey you're on has carried kings and queens. Legends are told about him."

Out of the corner of Zed's eye he caught sight of his stallion of a donkey, (stallion being the wrong word - feeble excuse of a donkey would be better). It wasn't the donkey's fault; he was just old. He'd been retired five years and was still coming to terms with being awoken from his afternoon nap and having a heavy saddle lumped rudely and without prior warning onto his back. He was not, therefore, very happy.

"Here you go Sir, jump on him."

"Are you positive about the 'jumping' and the 'on'? The phrase 'the straw that broke the camel's back' springs to mind. And no prizes for guessing who the straw is."

"Ah, he'll be fine Sir. The best we've ever had."

"Yeah, twenty years ago," Zed thought.

Carefully as he could, Zed mounted his ride. And instantly dismounted, although not through choice. He hadn't decided to de-mount and was as surprised as the stewardess, who he was now lying on, not to be on the donkey any more. As we said, the donkey was already annoyed and decided to take his anger out on Zed.

"Give him a carrot he'll be just fine then."

Zed bravely, after his near death experience, fed the beastly creature. And like all great animals, once fed, the donkey loved him. Up climbed Zed again and this time the donkey only creaked.

"Good donkey," said Zed more in hope than in praise.

Chapter Nineteen

The Devil knew that God knew that the Devil knew that God knew that he was up to something. Never one to shy away from bragging and much preferring to blow his own trumpet, he felt certain however that God knew nothing of his real plan.

Advisors, execs, portfolio managers and other clueless hell dwellers often invented intricately fiendish schemes against God but they always seemed to carry a risk that God would cease to exist. Now this was an almost insoluble dilemma. If the big man no longer existed, would anything else? Overrated yes, but being alive and existing has its perks. After several of these risky plans had been presented, the Devil had tried to emphasise that the basic requirement of a top plan was to still be alive at its conclusion. Did that stop them? No, if anything their hair-brained schemes became riskier and more absurd.

On a recent, mind-numbinggyly boring training course entitled 'Planning Made Simple the Mobster Way', that the Devil regretted booking onto, he noticed how effective kidnapping could be. Putting all his newly learnt planning schemes into action, he found a large whiteboard and grabbed the red pen. Making sure it was not a permanent marker, he wrote 'kidnap' and 'ransom'. He stood back, rested his pointy chin on his well-manicured hand and thought. Cautiously at first, he circled 'ransom', then with more vigour he circled 'kidnap' and confidently joined them together with a line. That was it. Kidnap someone and then ransom God for what he wanted.

Having created a plan of such simple elegant beauty, he felt convinced nothing would go amiss. Which is why he lectured to all that would listen that he was so peeved off that it had gone wrong! By now his demands should have been made and God would have a decision to make.

The situation required his best demon to be sent to rectify this sorry state of affairs. It was time to summon Botis. He needed to use the big guns as once Zed reached his parents the game was over. Or so he kept saying as often and loudly as possible.

Chapter Twenty

Picturesque, endless views of golden sand. Yet more stunning, uninterrupted, mind-bumbling bland views of sand. Free sand-blasting to toughen up any smoothness on your face and, at no extra cost, make your bum go numb and every bone in the body shake. Or at least that's how the donkey train brochure should read if you asked Zed.

Zed had lived a relatively privileged life so was more accustomed to first class cruising round the globe than sixth class journeys on a donkey's back. They had been going now for six hours with several stops at the desert service stations. Water, sandwiches and pick-n-mix was all they sold it seemed.

There comes a milestone in everyone's life when they reach a depressingly debilitating age that unfairly labels them as too old to buy pick-n-mix. Children have been produced, on more than one occasion, purely so their parents were once again able to pick the sweets they want and mix them in an overly priced bag to be weighed. For if you have a child with you, there is no shame.

Each stop on route crushed Zed's hopes of an alcohol-stocked pub. Annoyingly - and irresponsibly - one named 'The Desert Drinking Hole' raised his hopes high and he spent the rest of the journey working out ways to sue the place for false advertising. To state the painfully obvious, Zed was not enjoying himself. Hands tightly gripping his ride, still shaken after their first game of buckaroo, he sat gloomily staring at nothing in particular, as into the evening dusk and night sky they rode.

Majestically stunning views of twinkling stars that seem almost close enough to touch and the soothing sound of pure silence describes a desert sky at night back on earth. Black, featureless sky, the sound and smell of donkeys, and chilling air depicts it in heaven. Or at least it was where Zed found himself.

The train driver cried out for all to stop. Zed had felt no happiness in any way on his donkey adventure and felt a sense of relief hearing: "Everyone dismount their donkey. This is tonight's stop. Food and rooms are provided and dinner will be served promptly." They had stopped outside a gargantuan sized tent.

Swinging his leg over the donkey, Zed stretched the other out to find the safety of solid ground. If we rewind a second, the leg that had for all intents and purposes swung over, had in fact stayed rigidly firm on the other side. Hours of riding had seized up the muscles and, although Zed's brain thought the leg must have followed the instruction given, we now know it had not. Hence, when Zed went to put his weight on the other foot, his whole body tilted to one side, going further than his body's centre of gravity pulling the rest over with it. Zed fell off ungracefully and with a whimpering sound of an imbecile. Turning round to see what all the noise was about, his donkey gave a grunt acknowledging it had no more energy and promptly sat down.

"Arggggh!" cried Zed.

It had sat down on Zed. "Well he looked soft," reasoned the donkey, getting up, hoping Zed would be quieter. "Don't see what all the fuss is about, you sat on me all day and I sit on you for two seconds and you scream as though I've broken your legs. Bloody humans."

Wandering into the overly sized tent it didn't take Zed long to fathom out that by 'room' they meant sleeping bag with accompanying lumpy brown pillow. At least the food smelt good. Instantly recognisable to any food-loving nose, it was the traditional English dish known as a curry. Stolen from India and modified for the great bland taste buds of an Englishman. Wafting through the enormous tent, it would have made even the most devout monk break a hunger fast. Belly rumbling, mouth salivating, Zed left the disappointment of his 'room' in search of his evening feast. Located at the opposite end of the tent, Zed found a great, long wooden table filled all along the middle with overflowing pots of curry, naan breads, samosas, pakoras and the less traditional, but just as important, chips. People were filling their plates high making leaning towers with their food. Zed joined in and soon his belt required loosening a notch or two. The food was as tasty as it looked but not even these hungry travellers could wrestle down all the mountain of food provided.

The little amount of small talk that took place between shovelling food down hungry mouths led Zed to find he was not the only one looking for someone. Most of the train's passengers seemed to have been in heaven for several years and grown weary where they lived and had made the decision to re-acquaint themselves with their relatives – just like Zed. Others were keen historians exploring heaven to sample real people from the times they had researched and read about. All of them expressed their surprise on Zed's rash decision to go travelling from day one of heaven life.

"You left a bar? Dude if I'd been clever enough to design my dingo of a house with a bar I'd never have left."

"Oh really. Well maybe I was a bit rash but there was no hot water."

"Classic Pom, no patience. Utilities and furniture come the next day."

"Oh bother."

"Dude, if I were you I'd turn back now."

Zed expressed regret with a deep sigh. He stayed out of any further chat, not wanting to find other things to brood over.

With people finishing eating, Zed said his goodbyes and retired to his bag to sleep, he pondered again why he was so adamant about this parent thingy. The idea seemed to appear like a huge boulder in your garden overnight that you are unable to move the next day. Strange, he thought. Putting his head down he reminisced about his mum and dad. He remembered the last time he was with his dad in an old peoples' home. His dad had offered him some sound advice that he religiously observed to this day. "Son, never tip a hairdresser. Nurses, doctors, teachers - now that's who you should tip." A tear came to his eyes, but also a smile. Drifting off to sleep he wondered when and if he would see them again.

There is not much in the deserts of heaven; animals who spent their lives fighting the harsh environment to survive certainly were not found there in heaven. They were much more likely to be found in areas boasting unlimited water supplies and shade at each turn. Tonight though there was something. Lurking outside, slithering silently through the desert sand and heading with a hint of evil intent towards the service station tent was Botis.

Being the Great President of Hell meant he had certain responsibilities. Currently he was very annoyed; this business was getting in the way. He couldn't understand why the boss was so obsessed by this nobody. The Devil, no matter how hard he protested, just wouldn't listen when he pleaded not to send him this time; he was up to his eyes in overdue paperwork. After the Devil explained calmly that if he didn't go, then 'things may happen', he dutifully gave in and obeyed. Botis knew from experience that confrontation was best avoided when the Devil was involved.

Botis never felt at home or comfortable in heaven. It was fine when he was in snake form but when changing to a human shape he stuck out like a sore thumb. Being able to shape-shift your form at any time sounds great, and it can be. However, it also involves decades of boring repetitive practice. He'd never actually managed to master the human shape fully. The basics were there; some bits could be described as perfect but no matter how much he practised there was always two large horns sticking out of his head. Why this was, no one could explain. To hide the horns he tried many a disguise over the years and after much trial and error had settled on a hat. A stupidly-shaped, oversized hat at that. Possessing a demon's mind, Botis never fully understood the calamitous effect his hat made; it drew more attention than it distracted from his horns. People would mostly ridicule him when in heaven and that made him mad.

The boss's instructions or, more accurately, orders were to the point. Either stop this shit-for-brains Zed from meeting his parents, or else don't bother returning back to hell. As the elected President of Hell, he didn't think this task was for him. It seemed beneath his rank. But with a threat more threatening than a pure, filtered, extra strong threat itself, he lacked any other choices.

Botis, in current form, stretched out to a full three metres long; dark brown skin dotted with black stripes decorated the slimy body. Trapped along the muscular uncoiled snake body lay a deadly sword that, when unsheathed, turned Botis into a psychopathic killing machine. But for this job his more subtle powers of telling the future and past would be of more use.

Slithering round the back of the tent he found his victim waiting. Truth be told he was not waiting, more smoking like a naughty schoolboy behind the bike sheds. And the headmaster Botis had more than lines in mind for punishment! Moving silently but for the sound of a few sand particles moving obligingly from his path, he looked for his victim. Elliott enjoyed a smoke yet felt that in heaven it may be considered a sin. So ignoring the 'God is everywhere and sees all fact' he wrongly assumed no one would notice a quick smoke behind the tents. This guilt and the assumption he was alone exponentially increased Elliott's shock when he heard a voice behind him say 'hi'.

Jumping round, hiding his cigarette behind him, now in a complete state of God fearing 'oh no, I'm going to be sent to hell' state, his lips moving in readiness of the need to beg forgiveness. Yet to his surprise, no one was there.

His eyes sensed nothing and his ears told the brain to stand down and relax - a false alarm. The only problem came from the nose. It had no intention of relaxing. 'Panic,' it shouted. 'Water we need water.' The other two senses that through life always felt far superior told the nose to shut up.

Elliott was from the era of the horrendous fashion statement - the shell suit. A marvellously, dangerous design when around fires. The cigarette he had so swiftly concealed behind his back ignited the purple shell suit instantly, spreading faster than a bush fire.

Belatedly, accepting that the nose had a point, Elliott screamed. He ran and ran and ran. In no particular direction but within five minutes he was a mere flaming spot on the horizon. Botis, still watching bemused, laughed. "Humans," he thought, "absolute idiots. How does he not know that in heaven you don't feel pain? All he had to do was calmly put the fire out and that'd be that. Idiots."

Dispensing with this human was a necessary part of Botis's plan. Now came the tricky part, made doubly tricky due to Elliot bolting across the desert before he got a proper look at his face. The first step in his plan meant changing his form to look like Elliott. He needed to take his form so that he could blend in seamlessly with the group. Slowly his snake shape rose and grew wider, then shorter. Hands and legs appeared. His head became human and even his clothes were formed in a perfect shell suit copy. To watch this would be like seeing a clay model squashed and prodded, slowly being worked into its final shape. Stretching out his hands, turning them over, feeling his clothes, fingering his facial features, Botis could tell he'd done a fantastic job. Smiling he tested his walk. And then 'pop, pop', out came the bloody horns. "For fuck sake!" Hours of classes, hypnosis, back to basics, 'Human Body for Dummies', he'd tried them all and nothing worked. At least he'd brought his top hat.

Chapter Twenty One

After a much shorter, and appreciably more comfortable journey, Bob arrived in top spirits at his destination. He'd handed out flyers, preached and effectively become the least liked person aboard his train. He succeeded, as all barmy preachers do, (even with the odds piled high against him), to entice one gullible person to listen – long enough for a spot of brain washing. She could now recite all the stories of Zed the saviour, and considering Bob met Zed only twice, there was a hell of a lot to tell. Seeing greatness in his new recruit, Bob honoured her with speedy promotion to high priestess, and sent her to preach afar.

Leaving his assimilated subject to do his bidding, Bob punched the air with a quick right-left-right combination. Never back on earth had Bob revelled in this much fun. With a large smile and spirits high, he stepped out of the station and into Ancient Rome.

The entrance to Rome was a sight to behold and Bob beheld it in awe. A spectacular triumphal arch spanned a wide, marble road. The arch took in four entrances, each decorated with a majestic, stone statue of Roman soldiers sitting on horseback, guarding the paths beyond.

Some sandaled-cladded locals were minding their own business at the side of the road; Bob sprung on them and took his opportunity.

"Excuse me, young men, what a fine day it is. And such good taste you have in togas and sandals. Where would I find the centre of this great place, somewhere people gather and crowds form?"

Staring blankly at one another, not really understanding the question, the eldest of the group, noticing this guy was not from these parts, offered directions to where all tourists tended to visit. "If you follow this road straight ahead until you see the baths, then hang a straight for another few miles. Look out for the great theatre and then go straight and follow the road until you find the amphitheatre."

Digesting these tricky directions Bob concluded in a slow deliberate manner. "So what you're saying is go straight then straight and then straight again?"

"If you want, yes."

"Well thank you for sharing your knowledge. Now let me share mine."

Half an hour later Bob found himself in a jail of some sort listening to people arguing the merits of his crucifixion. To Bob's great surprise, not all Romans had a burning desire to hear of Zed; it perplexed and worried him when others appeared not so keen. Lesser men would panic, but Bob was not a lesser man. He wasn't a normal man either - just borderline mad.

"Crucify me, for all that hear about it will know my name. I mean Zed's name."

"Quiet, you blasphemous pig. There is only one saviour and his name is Jesus."

Genuinely confused Bob checked. "Hold on, didn't you guys crucify him?"

"Merely an administrative error for which we have apologised. And we don't need to apologise to you!"

Bob did what all mad preachers do and angered his captors further by reciting from the book of Zed. The room descended into chaos with threats of upside down crucifixion and other such horrors.

"Everyone be quiet!"

A tall, powerful woman with 'I'm in charge' authority about her and a booming voice burst through the door. Everyone fell silent.

"We've imprisoned an infidel, and will punish him in our traditional manner, if that's ok," said one of the men hiding behind a slightly taller guy.

"And what," said the commanding woman, "is our traditional punishment?"

The group of men previously so confident in front of their captured infidel started shifting around, nervously looking at each other. They pushed their leader to the front and looking at the floor he mumbled: "Crucifixion."

"What did you say? Say it louder."

"I said, ummm, crucifixion."

Grabbing the man by his ear, she dragged him effortlessly across the room to Bob. "Apologise to this man. You know we banned crucifixion after that paperwork mishap."

"Sorry," he murmured in a sheepish manner.

"Now let him go. What's your name?" she demanded staring directly at Bob in a not so friendly way, but higher up on the friendly scale than threatening crucifixion.

The crowd of men made their way out, apologising profusely on their way.

"I am Bob, I am here to teach to word of Zed."

Without missing a beat the scary woman didn't give Bob a chance. "That's splendid, but if you teach any word near me I'll teach you the word of pain."

Bob knew he was on to a loser with this one.

"Of course good lady. A favour to ask before I leave, which way to the amphitheatre and could you possibly release me from this cell?"

With a grin like a Cheshire cat she replied: "Say please."

"Please."

Her smile widened. "Now say pretty please, oh saviour."

She knew this would rattle him. Bob, just as the woman suspected, wrestled between the notion of calling anyone saviour apart from Zed and the chance of freedom, he failed to notice he'd already let himself out. Leaning on the unlocked door did the trick.

"Oh calm down Bob, you've released yourself."

Surprised, Bob fell to his knees and thanked God for releasing him.

"Get up fool. You don't need to thank him now you're in heaven. You've already done enough or the pearly gates would have slammed in your face."

"Garden gate."

"What?"

"They've down-sized the entrance to heaven; it's now a garden gate."

Not really understanding, she changed the subject. "Here are your directions to the amphitheatre. Listen carefully for I shall only say this once."

Bob bravely interrupted. "Just guessing, but is it straight then straight and maybe straight again?"

"Have you been there before? Stop wasting my time and go if you already know the way."

So off he trotted in a straight sort of direction, after thanking the lady for halting the crucifixion and all that.

It took a good hour of straight walking along the pure, polished, marble road to reach the amphitheatre. If he'd felt the need to touch the path then he'd have noticed the whole marble floor had under floor heating for no apparent reason - other than Romans will be Romans. Along the way Bob held a few impromptu, preaching sessions to practise before the big event. Astonishingly, four gullible women heard the call of a cult; Bob could see them follow him at a distance, hoping to hear more about this Zed chap. "They're mine," he thought smiling.

Chapter Twenty Two

Full to the brim with curry, Zed waddled off to find his room. Cunningly, Zed knew he must collapse into bed early to get up even earlier. Any place that used the unfortunate words 'communal showers' required forward planning to be the first to use them. Drifting off into the land of nod, he dreamed of the days when his bottom felt pleasantly normal.

Rising at the crack of dawn, Zed quietly slipped from his sleeping bag and headed for the showers - which if lady luck was on his side today - would be clean. What he failed to notice were the empty sleeping bags around him.

Approaching the showers, silent as a slug stalks its next leaf, (so as to not wake the shower thieves), Zed opened the door and entered the wet room. At this point Zed realised he was not the first but more likely the last to use it this morning. (Somehow his plan had failed before it even started.) The room was revolting. It stunk to high heaven and was floating in a sea of mud, sand and perhaps water. Exhaling a deep moan, he made his way to an empty shower and freshened up as best he could. A bad workman always blames his tools, and Zed was adamant about blaming the tools provided here. The shower turned out to be solar powered which, on pure principals, was stupid. During the day a solar shower kicked out heat powerful enough to kill a cockroach. Now in the early hours the solar shower had no power so was ……

"Ahhhhhhh!"

For the second time in Zed's short stay in heaven, freezing cold water pummelled his naked body. Not an angry man on normal occasions, Zed was pushed over his limit and made a mental note to write a poor review in the guest book. He also wondered how a solar shower worked without a sun.

After drying with the brown (yet once white), wet, used towels, he re-applied his clothes. Like a toilet roll dipped into water, the clothes sucked up the un-dried water from Zed's body so now, although he was dry, his clothes were soaking. "What a nightmare," he thought moodily. "More hell than heaven at the moment."

It's at times like this that you rely on one's brain to think thoughts to warm the soul, to rekindle some joy or just to find a pub. Zed, being Zed, would have chosen the pub but his brain whizzed into action and came up with a pub-topping scheme. Get your lazy, wet arse up to the train and be first to board. You'll have the pick of the donkeys. No time to waste, he made a dash for the exit. Ahead he could see everyone, still zombies in their sleep-deprived state, herding themselves like sheep to the donkeys. Not usually one to gloat, Zed's brain couldn't help itself. "Ha! Look at you all," it thought. "When I reach the queue to board first, one of you suckers will have to ride on the retired donkey. Not me today though." Increasing his speed, Zed motored on and could have reached speeds Zed had never reached before if he wasn't being slightly impeded by sand sticking to his wet clothes.

Reaching his destination, the boarding master looked at him with some concern.

"You alright there mate? Do you have asthma?"

"No," Zed managed on the fourth attempt at speaking. "Just tell me, can I board now?"

"You bet your bottom dollar you can mate. The quicker you lot board, the quicker I finish for the day."

Almost knocking the boarding master over in his haste, Zed galloped to a prime specimen of a donkey and started to mount. Scrambling on, he sat on the finest donkey he could find and felt the soft, cosy, plush back he would now enjoy riding. Smiling, he eyed his fellow passengers with evil glee, watching the unfortunate losers arrive. Who would get the short-straw ride on his old donkey?

The boarding guard then delivered some earth shattering news.

"Attention all. Everyone mount your donkeys. Make sure it's the same one as yesterday."

"Oh bugger," Zed muttered as he dismounted slowly and made his way down to his not so favourite donkey. "Maybe it won't be quite so bad today," he thought, clinging on to this tiny hope as he mounted.

Twenty minutes into the journey his buttocks had gone from being numb to being in agony and yet still numb - which technically is a state that is impossible to achieve for one should cancel the other. To make matters worse, the passenger in front had spun round and was insisting on chatting to him while riding backwards. Attempts to ignore this chap proved fruitless; it's impossible to blank someone facing directly at you - and with only sand to stare at there seemed little chance of ignoring him.

Answering with a 'yes' or 'no' and occasionally a grunt, he did his best not to listen. Annoyance subsided while his brain tried to deduce the answer to a mystery, for Zed was perplexed as to where this backwards seated man had acquired such a tall hat. He certainly wore no head garments the previous day and there was no possible way he would forget a hat such as this. There were definitely no shops where they slept, and they hadn't yet reached the service station. So where the hat was from, Zed could not fathom.

He introduced himself as Botis. Clearly his parents called him that out of spite. Botis the Otis is what his brain wanted to call him. The guy, to be blunt, was strange. But most people in heaven appeared to be on the stranger side of the strange scale. "Does that mean I'm strange as well, or am I strange to think they're strange in a strange sort of Groundhog Day way?"

Unable to concentrate his brain on the 'strange' scale for long, Zed's thoughts were interrupted by an annoying tendency of Botis to end each sentence with a hissing sound. And the guy kept flicking his tongue in an unnerving way.

All Botis spoke of was the future. To Zed the future had not happened yet, and if it hadn't happened then there's certainly no need to worry or think about it. For Zed it was the past that worried him, a constant cause of embarrassment, remembering what ideally would be nice to forget. No, the future was none of his concern. Attempting to explain this to Botis proved pointless; no matter how many times the subject was changed the man kept jabbering on about it.

"Well if I have to exchange words with him I'm bloody well going to find out about his hat," thought Zed. "Listen here chappy, where did you acquire your fine hat? I knew a smashing gentleman years ago who always wore a tall hat but never have I seen such a unique specimen as yours. It's amazing it stays on."

"What, this hat?" Botis said, surprised that anyone would notice his incognito horn camouflage apparatus. "Had it with me all the time. Didn't you notice it yesterday?"

Keeping to Zed's more normal line of thoughts, his brain rationalised the answer so as not to confuse himself too much. "Must be the heat. How could I have not noticed that preposterous thing yesterday?!" he thought.

Botis returned the conversation to his topic of choice. "Have you ever met a person of mystic powers? One who can read your past and tell your future?"

"Oh God, here he goes again." Making one last attempt, Zed asked: "So was the hat tailored for yourself?"

"Never mind about my bloody hat. I've forgotten where I purchased the damn thing. Answer my question. It's vital you listen."

"Well yes I've heard of them. They seem to always be found in holiday resort type places. Pesky blighters they are too."

Springing into action, Botis stretched his neck forward and peered deep into Zed's eyes. "Would you like to know your future?" The world around Zed slowed down, like the start of an LSD induced trip. The air moved in ripples, objects wobbled in a rhythmic way and colours turned fluorescent. But Zed noticed none of this and asked: "Not just now thanks. If you can see the past then can you not look deep into it and find from whence came your hat?"

The world snapped back to normal with a twang. "Just forget about my fucking hat alright! Now let's do this the traditional way. Look at me Zed, look deep into my eyes."

The air again rippled, the sand turned pink, all the donkeys appeared to be flying and this time Zed's gaze was locked into Botis's large, round, snake's eyes. "I will take you on a journey deep into your past. Allow your mind to remember all that I tell. In the year of your tenth birthday, on a school trip to Wales, your teacher delivered some earth shattering news. Wales was not in fact a whale that people lived on. You had given a ten-minute presentation on how they shower in the whale's blowhole and other ridiculous theories. The whole class laughed and you cried for your mummy like a baby."

Not only could he remember this tragic moment in his life but also it now felt vividly real as though he was reliving it.

"Do you still remember that time?"

"Yes," Zed replied in a far-off sounding, trance-like voice.

"Let's take you somewhere else. Now remember this? The poor goat was having a nice day until you showed up. What happened next? I'll tell you."

Snapping out of the trance, Zed waved his hands in desperation and almost fell off his donkey shouting, "Not the goat, I don't want to think about the goat."

Demons do not have a sense of humour but seeing Zed's reaction almost brought laughter to Botis. "Calm your goat skin boots down. I'm not going to."

"Good."

Botis did know how to wind humans up, though.

"Any chance you have a goat – sorry, I mean coat - I could borrow?"

"Shut up."

"Sorry. This train is slower than a goat. Crap, I've done it again, I mean boat not goat."

"If you don't shut up now I'll ram your hat down your goat. Arghhhhh, I mean throat."

"I'm done, honest. I just needed to show you I can tell you the past. It seemed before you didn't believe in my powers; almost as though you had no interest."

Zed's brain had been on autopilot for the last half hour. No need to be in race gear when plodding along in this monotonous desert. When required though, brains can change gear at supersonic speeds. "He's just told my past," it thought. "Oh jeez I hope he doesn't know everything."

"How the Scooby do you know all this? Have you watched me from heaven while I grew up? Stalking is not allowed where I come from."

"I do not need to stalk. I have powers. Now behold your future."

Looking through Zed's eyes, focusing on the back of his head, the demon produced another one of his tricks. The air swirled up around Zed, blurring everything apart from Botis. The hairs on Zed's neck stood to attention, sweat dripped as though the sweat tap was on full. Attempting to lift his arms, he struggled to move. His whole body felt heavy. It was like trying to swim in treacle.

"I know all your past Zed and I can see all your future. The future for you has two paths." Being the showman, Botis fired up some pyrotechnics and explosions for dramatic effect. "Follow the right path and your time in heaven will be joyful; follow the other and it'll be awful." Botis paused, congratulating himself on his little rhyme. "Would you like to see the vision of your future paths?"

Zed's lips quivered like a Mexican wave being performed across his mouth. With all his effort he just managed to say, yes.

"The future I will tell you now, is the one that you are travelling along. The journey to your parents will be fraught with danger and pain. You will wander for years with no hope, finally meeting your parents and for what? Let me show you."

Botis set off the smoke machine he'd cunningly concealed. Pleased with its extra effect, he carried on.

"Observe the consequences of this foolish journey."

Everything disappeared and all that was left was darkness. "Oh bugger, hold on. Just gotta find something. Bloody darkness. Ah, here we are." And there in front of Zed he could clearly see himself and his parents. Strangely no one seemed happy.

"Look at the moment you long for in your thoughts. In your mind this is a joyful occasion but your mind imagines it wrongly."

No matter how Zed's brain decoded the images in front of him, it always came back with an annoying conclusion. They were all arguing, Zed shouting, his mum crying and his dad angry.

"Look, see how they despise you. For decades you try to find them. Do they appreciate it? On the contrary they hate you for it. They want you gone. Their heaven is heaven without you and they have no room to let you in."

Zed didn't know if he was confused, angry, upset or all three at once.

Smiling and watching Zed's baffled expression, Botis knew he'd had enough. "Away with you," the demon shouted; once again they were thrown into darkness.

"When I get back I'm returning this stupid machine, er, I mean the things you've just witnessed, are not set in stone. Follow your other path and this is what you'll see."

A new vision appeared plunging them into light again. Rubbing his eyes to adjust from darkness to strobe lighting, Zed slowly realised where he was. There, agonisingly close, was his beautifully crafted bar. Zed looked at the future Zed and how happy he appeared. There were even, what looked like, friends mingling away enjoying his hospitality.

"Ah my bar! How I miss her - we didn't have time to get to know each other," he said out loud.

Pulling Zed from the bar, the demon looked deep into his eyes. "This is the road you must take for happiness. Don't take the road to sadness." Holding on to Zed for a few more seconds, he clicked his fingers and Botis was gone. The bleak endless desert replaced his vision and his should-be-retired donkey was still plodding along oblivious to what Zed had just witnessed. One thing had changed though, the man in front along with his hat, no longer existed. They were gone, vanished.

"Well stranger things have happened to me," Zed thought. "Hang on. No they haven't!"

Chapter Twenty Three

Blood, guts, lions fighting bears, and other such grotesquely barbaric acts were the sort of entertainment Bob assumed he would be seeing at a Roman amphitheatre. Joining a herd of people flowing into the amphitheatre, Bob made his way to a free seat, sat back in reserved excitement ready for the first animal to be needlessly slaughtered. All started as envisaged. Out came a Hercules-bodied gladiator with glistening armour, oiled and tanned muscular body and a deadly looking Roman sword. Swinging his weapon in a manner that suggested he'd honed his skills at the finest sword swinging school, he slashed the air a couple of times before thrusting it skywards and slowly spun around surveying his adoring crowd. The elderly, over excited lady next to Bob nudged him and shouted over the cheers of the crowd: "He's going to fight a lion!"

"Fantastic," Bob thought. Hearing a huge roar, Bob craned his neck forward attempting to see a glimpse of the feared majestic creature over the frenzied crowd. Out came the lion. It didn't bound out in rage, nor did it come out slowly, stalking its prey. There was no King of the Jungle, Ruler of the Serengeti roar or snarling teeth dripping in angry saliva.

"Strange," thought Bob "why are two men pushing the lion from behind? A bit cruel to send out an injured lion." Then Bob realised the king of the jungle wasn't a lion; it was a two-dimensional, wooden cut-out, painted crudely to resemble a lion.

Like most ignorant humans, Bob failed to realise there are no animals in the Roman zone. There are very few in heaven and they mostly occupy areas where humans are not found. For to most animals, humans are the real demons. They torture, kill, force slave labour on them or generally tend to be mean. Sharing earth with them was hell. Why would a lion's or a bear's paradise include people who killed them for fun? The odd cat or dog may decide to live with humans in heaven - but only a rare few.

Bob watched in fascinated amazement as the slaughter of this wooden lion unfolded. Slashing, stabbing and diving heroically to avoid a choreographed lunge by the slow moving wooden beast. People even threw red paint each time the lion was stabbed. Eventually it was put out of its misery and lay on its painted side, dead as a doorknob while the gladiator lapped up the cheers and shouts from the crowd. A brave gladiator had risked his life knowing that one touch from the lion could have inflicted a mildly painful splinter. Even Androcles could not have saved the battered wooden lion but he could have helped any wounded gladiator with his expertise at splinter removals.

Leaning across to the woman who spoke earlier Bob asked: "What happens now?"

"Well, in the good old days on earth they would send out some prisoners to fight and be brutally killed by the gladiators, but alas now they play this game called football."

"Football?"

"Yes, a wanderer from another zone taught us the game, insisting that, being Roman Italians, we should be pretty good. One day he said there would be a heaven World Cup, but we aren't sure what that is."

"Football?" Bob said again. "Not football." Like a lot of men who have for years pretended to like football and had to put up playing it through their childhood as all the other boys did, when they hit adulthood they grew to detest the game.

"I'm not having bloody football!" And with that battle cry still echoing in the lady's ear he started fighting his way through the crowd. Being a wimpy sort of guy he didn't get far. His brain in all its excitement had forgotten he wasn't six feet tall and was on the plump side of the plump scale - attributes which detracted from his ability to pass through small gaps in the tightly packed crowd. Instead, he politely tapped shoulders asking if he could possibly, if no bother, make his way past, with 'pleases' and 'thanks' galore.

Twenty minutes into the game and the score was 1:0 (and would no doubt have gone 2:0 with Filippo del Totti being clean through on goal), the bemused referee blew his whistle to halt the game.

"Hey you, get off the pitch. I demand you get off this instant!"

With the referee shouting at him, Bob ran past a long haired, six feet tall, muscularly built player and accidentally made the merest of physical contact, brushing his clothes against the guy's hand.

"Ahhhh!" screamed the player diving to the floor rolling over three times and clutching his untouched knee in agony. "Not noticing he'd nearly 'killed' a player, who miraculously recovered within two minutes after being stretchered off, Bob carried on regardless and confronted the confused but angry referee.

"Listen here, I am Bob and command you to step aside. I have been sent from the chosen one."

This forceful statement hit the referee hard. Ever since the Romans accidentally, after a mistake with paperwork, crucified the saviour of earth, son of the creator, fish and wine extraordinaire and all round top chap, they became very wary and cautious in certain situations. With Bob mentioning - with what sounded like some authority - the words 'chosen one', Mr Referee decided to step aside. "No point risking anything," his brain sensibly reasoned.

The hundred thousand strong crowd fell silent looking on in confused amazement as Bob took centre stage. Slowly he turned a full 360 degrees, mirroring the gladiator, eyeing up his crowd. Ideally he would have preferred a microphone, stage lights and big screen - perhaps even some intro music. But this would do for now. Raising his hand in a symbolic gesture, he went full throttle into his rhetoric about Zed.

For all his failings, you had to admire his ability to hold a crowd while preaching. People gasped and cheered, even at points shedding tears. By the end, his whole body was close to collapse. Some of the players rushed to his side and helped him back into the home changing rooms.

Bob, although physically exhausted, radiated a glow of happiness around him. He had come, seen and conquered. (When in Rome and all that.)

There would be thousands whom he commanded now; many had already spread around heaven, preaching and enticing others to join. If all roads lead to Rome, then there was a road to everywhere from Rome for his devoted followers to follow. He lay back on the wooden bench and smiled. "They love me," he thought - and went to sleep.

Chapter Twenty Four

Surrounded by the Princes, Dukes and project managers of hell, the Devil was growing impatient waiting for Botis. Lateness infuriated him and Botis being late was made doubly worse with his present company. Botis was due to make his presentation on The Zed Project and thus was holding up the rest of his meeting. All were seated around a beautifully crafted, dark wooden table that oozed evil. The Devil banged his fist down making everything on the table jump in the air. This promptly brought silence to the room.

"Look," said one of the senior Princes, "if he doesn't turn up soon we'll just move on to the next point on the agenda. We have heard numerous complaints about the whips being used. There is a motion being brought by the hell workers' union, that the barbed wire whips be replaced by a more humane punishment."

The Devil almost choked on his triangular cucumber sandwich. "They say what?!"

"They've handed in a petition with a few million signatures claiming that the whip is an out-dated form of punishment and a more humane torture device should be used. Examples they gave were: no cake after tea, or stand in the corner with a pointy hat on."

"To be clear... they want a more humane punishment dealt out to them when in hell?"

A few around the table nodded at the Devil.

"Tell them to go fuck themselves. Who do they think they bloody are? In my mum's day, being whipped by barbed wire whips was a light punishment. They should be thankful the crocodile crotch clamp has been outlawed. Anyway what are they going to do if I say no to the mortal schmucks?"

"Strike, sir."

This time it was a great goblet full of red wine that got some physical punishment from the Devil. Smashing against the dark oak panelled wall, the wine ran down - and a keen observer might have noticed the blood like consistency.

"Strike?! They can't do that!"

"Actually they can. The union fought for that last year and it's now law."

The Devil sank back into his throne. "What is becoming of my kingdom," he thought giving a heavy sigh. It was at this point Botis arrived.

"Ah Botis," said the clerk, "we will go back to point one on our agenda if you are ready."

"I'm ready and bring great news. As expected I have successfully planted the seed in Zed's brain - going on his silly excursion will only bring disappointment. Now as we speak, he travels across the desert. And in that bleak environment, he's only the thoughts and images planted in his minute human brain to mull over for hours on end; the seed that I have sown will grow. Soon the seed will become a rain forest and he will return home."

"Well done Botis. At last, some progress." The Devil sat upright in his chair again. "Now bring me a whip, some barbed wire and anyone who has threatened to strike. I make the fucking rules round here, not some pathetic sinners from Earth!"

Botis wandered home to his pit in hell, happy that he had pleased the master. This could result in a bonus or even a promotion. Just one thing he couldn't understand, why was the boss so obsessed with stopping Zed getting to his parents?

Chapter Twenty Five

Not everyone knows, or even agrees, that Angels are considerably smarter than the average bear and a lot smarter than humans. From the moment Elemiah first had the misfortune of meeting Zed she perceived danger. Now, hovering high above a bleak desert with only a donkey train breaking the monotony of sand, her theory certainly appeared to be cemented into proof. First the house attack by that meddling Xaphan, and now in full daylight Botis the Otis was up to his old tricks again. Directly overhead of the Otis she watched as he attempted to impede Zed's journey with emotional confusion. "One trick pony that Botis," she thought, "but it's served him well so why change now."

Unlike the humans with badly made, inferior human eyes, Elemiah could see everything that Botis projected to Zed. "I'll admit that he has certainly mastered this vision illusion," she mused. "Any dumb human let alone the brightest ones would fall for his treachery. Zed will be changing his mind and heading back to his home soon. Damn it!" Half panicking but still just about able to still think straight she knew something must be done.

But what, and why? For she knew Zed must meet his parents but the why still refused to be decoded. There seemed no suggestion God was attempting to help Zed or prevent the Devil interfering in heaven. It was just like the old days when God and the Devil constantly played out these games to test each other. Was this an attempt to destroy heaven again or maybe take over heaven? "God knows," she thought. And He probably did.

Chapter Twenty Six

Riding along on his donkey of a donkey, Zed reminisced about the good old days. There was a time when his body owned a bum. Without doubt, before this journey, there was a bottom where one should be. Alas though, now it was no longer there. He couldn't feel it. There was no pain from either buttock. Whacking or pinching it produced no response from any pain receptors. So in purely physiological terms it ceased to exist. In the physical realm, if you cannot feel something, does it exist? Admittedly, if there were to be a handy mirror wandering around this bleak desert, then a quick glance at his derriere would disprove this theory. It would also bring on a new hypothesis about donkey trains flattening bums - actually not so much flat but more concave. The bum curve was now going in the wrong direction. To amplify the indignation of losing his bum, he was equally incensed that he had lost it for no reason.

"What's the point in locating the old man and mother if they no longer love me?"

To amplify what was already amplified, he knew that to venture back to his beloved bar he'd have to go through the pain of the bum-losing donkeys again. Staring accusingly at his ride having a well-deserved drink, Zed set about looking for a bar to wet his whistle in the donkey station they'd just arrived at.

Breathing in sand, staring at nothing but sand and occasionally emptying the sand out of one's underwear had caused Zed's brain to go off the boil slightly. So it took him a good fifteen minutes to acknowledge what was said upon dismounting. This was the end of the line, no more donkey pain, no more sand. A rush of guilt shot through his body for not saying 'bye' to his desert companion. Hate and anger is all he felt for the poor retired animal but a bond was built between the two through mutual hatred, a bond that deserved a goodbye. For one fleeting second he thought about running off and flinging his arms around his old donkey in a hug, but the urge for a drink outweighed this quickly forgotten thought.

Stopping to get his bearings, Zed scanned his surroundings. They had arrived at a station throbbing with activity; people rushing to catch their train, others waiting for loved ones to arrive and all around stalls selling everything from the exotic to the erotic. The most striking feature about the stalls and surrounding buildings was their shape - it stood out like a sore thumb. Everything here seemed to be built with one shape in mind - a pyramid.

Zed had been too busy brooding on his anger issues to remember his final destination. Anyone walking out of the station's exit would be entering what was weirdly called the Egyptian zone. Now, how a country – Egypt - was a time in history, no one was sure, but as mentioned before, God's design of heaven was not subject to planning regs. so was essentially random.

Drifting teasingly, riding on ripples in the air, came smells of spices. Spices that had been expertly sprinkled over marinated chicken and cooked on a skewer to perfection. The smell made its way up Zed's nostrils and caught by hairs housing thousands of smell receptors each sending 'come eat me' messages direct to his brain. This produced hunger rumbles in his stomach, making it perfectly clear that anything apart from finding food was unacceptable. Not one to waste time, he chose the first pyramid food hut that he came to. As a youth he'd wasted many an hour with his chums wandering past pub after pub until the correct one to drink in was agreed upon. Why, he always thought, not just go into the first one you see? The quicker you are in, the sooner a drink can be in your hand. Since those dark days he'd vowed never to waste time like that again.

This particular food joint, (which happened to be the closest), was constructed from stone and shaped like a pyramid that had been chopped in half from the top down. All the stones appeared to be different sizes and, if a passing big bad wolf happened to huff and puff, the whole thing was in danger of coming tumbling down. Since this time zone of heaven was a thousand odd years older than Zed, the man serving food dressed to match the time period. He wore a fitted white - or what was once white - tunic with a brightly decorated belt. Zed did not, and so stuck out like a blue whale going about its business in the Sahara.

"Ah, man from long way away what would you like?" The trader had a gruff sounding voice, one that is only acquired through years of sanding the lining of your throat. Ending his sentence he spat some spit onto the floor near Zed's shoe.

Instantly questioning his decision on where to eat and with high suspicions of food hygiene and safety practices, he went to ask for the guy's food safety certificate. His brain had a brief argument with itself; after weighing up this worry, it concluded that the fear of spit in the food was less than the pain of having to find somewhere else to eat.

"Howdy, what fine treats do you have to offer? Is there a menu? Oh bother I won't be able to read it will I as you chaps use those hieroglyphics."

The guy rolled his eyes and sniggered while still spitting at every opportunity. "Hey Ahmose. We've got another plonker here. Thinks we write in pictures, the muppet." Both men spat in recognition of this hilarious event.

The other guy slapped his forehead and shook his head. "From the future again is he?"

"Sorry to interrupt your heckling of me, are you saying you don't use hieroglyphics? Not to be rude but I've seen it in books. My old history master taught us boys all about it. You left conclusive evidence about the place that we have researched and translated."

"You talking about what's his name. Hey Ahmose. What's that guy's name that came here saying he'd worked our language out?"

"Oh you mean Jean."

"Yes that's the fella."

The mention of Jean caused a large amount of spitting by everyone who heard. "Is this how the Nile gets its water source?" thought Zed. " A whole river and city created from spit."

"Jean? Jean Francois Champollion? We learnt all about him. Spent his life working your language out. Did he come here then?" continued Zed.

"Yep. He came here. Wandered into our part of heaven all cocky and asking stupid questions. When he learnt that what he thought was our language was just kids' picture books he flipped. Spent a whole day staring at the floor muttering to himself; then the next day he stripped naked covered himself in pictures and ran through the streets telling everyone that they knew nothing and this is our language. Well we didn't put up with it, so strapped him to the next donkey train and sent him packing. That's the last we ever heard from him."

"Good grief."

"We laugh about it now but at the time we were peeved off."

"Well I never. Poor chap. Would cost a heap of money to change all the history textbooks. Best to keep the truth quiet for now. Next you will tell me old Kippers in year ten was giving us false information about thousands of slaves being whipped day and night to build the great pyramids."

The guy's face wrinkled up and you could see a shot of pain go through his body. "We don't like to remember all that."

"So the old boy was right when he scared us in class. Once, when Fredders my old mate pulled a prank on Kippers, he threatened to whip him into an Egyptian."

Visibly angered, the stall owner butted in. "No one could convey the pain we went through to build those stupid pyramids. Woken up each morning at five, we didn't wash with water but had the dirt whipped from our bodies. Then they made us wear stupid clothes followed by a full day of more whipping at work. On a good day we'd stop for occasional breaks so the masters could whip us for having a break that they made us have."

"Sounds like a whip roaring time."

"Listen here you infidel." The guy grabbed Zed by the neck and pulled his face next to his. Zed prayed he would not spit being this close to his mouth. "You dare to make a joke about this?"

"Sorry, sorry. It's my brain's fault. Didn't consult me before saying those words."

"Well we Egyptians know how to pull a brain out through your nose so you tell your brain to shut it. Ok?"

"Yes of course. Would be my pleasure."

Seeing the guy calm down slightly, Zed tried to engage him in less controversial conversation.

"Did any of the Pharaohs make it to heaven?"

"No! You can't kill thousands of innocents and come here. We even heard that when they go to hell the Devil tricks them into thinking they are in the paradise they believed they would ascend to. All their gold and slaves are with them - just as the afterlife was predicted. But then the gold turns to excrement and the slaves turn to demons - and then they know. They know that they were diabolical on earth and in death they will suffer."

"I don't mean to be rude," conscious that any wrong words could be the last the brain hears "but if all this brings back such bad memories why do you build all the buildings pyramid shaped?"

"Status of course. It's engraved in our culture, the bigger the pyramid the more important you are. Even though you hate the person at the top you still want to be him."

"True," thought Zed. "I always hated Godfrey, my old boss, but I still became one. "

Zed ordered an Egyptian kebab and sat down to munch it while contemplating life - or death as it more technically was. Zed's choice of seat overlooked - from quite a height - the ancient Egyptian heaven settlement. And quite a view it was to behold. Pyramid after pyramid after sphinx. Running right through the middle was, of course, a great river that looked too clean to be saliva based.

Zed often liked to be alone in his thoughts and heaven weighed heavily on his mind. Different religions provided alternative visions of heaven - and from what he had seen so far they all appeared wrong. Not one to have questioned what heaven would be like while alive, he now realised no one had addressed the main points. Firstly, why has no scholar theorised about the infrastructure in heaven? Some clever chappy surely must have questioned that if there a billions upon billions of people are up there, then where do they all live - and what about transport? Zed found himself getting angry with God. Why did he not organise heaven to place newcomers with their family?

"Good day, man with charming face."

Startled by a woman shouting this at him Zed sprang to his feet in a defensive manner. His body poised at any moment to do what any beta male would do and leg it as fast and cowardly as possible.

"Do not be alarmed, I come offering a great tour of the Egyptian land."

"That's a delightful offer madam but I would prefer to be left alone." Turning around he attempted to make it clear he wanted to be alone.

"Do not turn down my offer so quickly. This is a once-in-heaven, eternal, lifetime opportunity. Normally I am fully booked up all year but I could see on your face you needed something to take your mind off the troubles in your eyes."

Looking at the woman, Zed's subconscious part of his brain was hammering on the conscious side and the message was just getting through.

"Don't I know you from somewhere?" was the message, but like a Chinese whisper it came out as: "Why are you not spitting?"

"I'm sorry, what did you say, spitting?"

"Yes, everyone I have met in this pyramid themed zone spit as though it's as natural as breathing."

"You must have not seen me spit, Zed."

And with great effort and several attempts the female guide spat on the floor.

"How do you know my name?"

"You told me."

"No I didn't."

"Yes you did."

"No. I would recall telling you as we have only chatted for five minutes."

"Well, I'm Egyptian."

"And that's relevant how?"

"Everyone knows Egyptians can guess a man's name from a hundred yards."

"And a woman?"

"Oh seventy yards."

One of the most over-used parts of Zed's brain was the: 'can't be bothered to argue' part, and once again it decided to act decisively and just accept this as fact.

"Yes, I'm sure I heard that somewhere once."

Hunched over, the woman looked quite elderly but appeared to have no problems moving about. You could tell that in her youth she would have stood tall as a powerful woman. She was wearing what appeared to be bed sheets tied up with a tatty old rope and sporting more modern looking shoes that clashed with her outfit.

"Follow me Zed and you will be amazed." She echoed the word amazed and brought the word to life. No one could resist that. Some people have a gift with speech and can make even a description of a blade of grass sound like an exquisitely exciting enigma of ecstasy itself. The way this old lady voiced the sentence not only affected Zed, even the sand wanted to follow her.

"Oh, alright then. But will there be much walking?"

Chapter Twenty Seven

Somewhere in the forests of the lost tribes, deep in the heart of heaven's interlocking zones, a petite, light brown, speckled winged butterfly flapped its tiny delicate wings. The air around whooshed and swirled. To a human it was not visible just a pin drop in the air's ocean, but from the tiniest seed a giant can grow. The minute wind roamed around for hours on end until it met more tiny winds from other butterfly wings. Some of the butterflies were also brown, some white while others had flamboyantly decorated wings - yet they all produced the same puff of wind from their small delicate wings. Slowly the winds joined forces, like an invisible attraction squashing and squeezing the winds together. Growing ever so slowly, the winds gathered enough energy for a weatherman to declare a light breeze, but still it grew and as it grew it became angrier.

Chapter Twenty Eight

Chilling in his fire of doom, Satan worked on his next move. Living in a land full of fire, it would surprise some to know that the Devil had a log burner installed in every room. A recent arrival - an interior designer - advised the Devil it was all the rage; keen to keep up with the latest fashions, he had them fitted in as many rooms as possible. He poked the fire to get it going and tossed another screaming sinner's head in. Botis had performed exceedingly well, and Zed would be returning to his comfy home soon. "What to do now?" he said out loud while rubbing his pointy, evil, freshly shaved red chin. "Let's get them to conjure up a plan to trap and bring Zed down below to bathe in the flames of hell." Realising he'd exclaimed this sentence loudly and dramatically, he went red with embarrassment. No one could tell though, as he was red, red like a tomato, an embarrassed, evil tomato. Should he send a few legions of demons and purely overpower him? Or would it be more fun and exciting to lay a cunning devilish trap? He reached for what looked like a ram's horn attached to wires that had been blackened by the flames of hell itself (which of course is what had happened) and spoke into it with his best shop assistant voice.

"This is your leader, bringer of doom, nightmare of nightmares, the maker of darkness.... Could all exec. members of the elite trapping team report to the wasp room - formally known as meeting room four. Anyone late will be asked to attend this evening's class in the snake pit. Goodbye and have a good day. Bing"

The most recent project manager to arrive in hell - for hell is where they go, each year increasing their numbers exponentially - had keenly informed Satan of the latest business fad to name meeting rooms. Impressed by this, Satan had excitedly renamed all his rooms after animals. Imagining that his hell meeting rooms were now modern and hip, the deflating news about his incorrect choice of names had been a blow. Why name them after cities or tube stations when animals rock? This rash project manager is now embedded in nails within a room of nails embedded in lava made from molten metal melted nails.

The six execs. were waiting in the wasp room, PowerPoint presentations at the ready and laser pens fully charged. Each one was eager to be chosen, all were ready to dismiss their competitors' plans as nonsense. They agreed only one thing, they need at least four meetings a day, allowing only ten minutes for actual work to be carried out. They had a brief to present a plan to trap Zed on his house return.

"Good evening, gentlemen. Coffee and biscuits are due soon but for now you may start."

Going round the room, ideas ranged from a large hole covered by the doormat for him to fall through, to elaborate plans stolen from books they'd read in the past. An hour into the meeting the Devil snapped.

"You lot make the crap on my shoe look like intelligent dolphins! I wanted originality, not the same old shit people have used over and over. We need to make a point to God. He needs to see our genius." Pointing at the one remaining dweeb not to outline his plan yet. "You. Give me your plan now!"

Standing up, the project managing dweeb looked a frail man. Sporting horrendous glasses, bowler head haircut, quite short and dressed in a suit with legs that hung too long and sleeves that were cut too short. Not the look associated with most evil spirits consigned to the pit of hell.

"Your sire, I propose a three point attack." He spoke with an evil cackle, always looking at the floor, only making eye contact on rare occasions. " We have already created for Zed the house of his dreams. Now we need a garden to match. While he travels through the desert, we shall fill his garden with the joys of his youth. We need the pond he caught frogs in, the bike he rode on and any other joyful things that bring back fond memories as a boy. But most importantly we need an apple tree."

Looking up half bemused and half angered, the Devil considered what was said. "An apple tree? This plan had best improve rapidly before I make you never want to see an apple tree again!"

"Please sire, I promise the plan improves. The apple tree is vital to the plan. It is the tree he climbed for fun years ago, the tree he would hide in when his parents called him to dinner, and the tree he would cry in when upset."

"Enough about the bloody tree. How will you trap Zed?"

"Ah well you see, that involves the tree."

"Go on then."

"I can not."

"I said get on with it!" The Devil spat out his words in anger.

"But I protest sire, I am forbidden."

"Either you carry on now or I will carry you into a life of pain."

"But you instructed me not to talk about the tree."

"AND?" The Devil loomed over the cowering exec.

"Well, if you want me to carry on with the plan I need to talk about the tree."

"Oh for fuck sake, you can talk about your bloody tree, just hurry up." He slouched back into his chair already giving up any hope that the plan may be ingenious or cunning or even average.

Looking timid, the dweeb continued with his plan. "Once the garden has been created, not forgetting the apple tree at the centre, we will wait for Zed to return. He will arrive home and head straight for his beloved bar at the bottom of his garden. "But wait, what is this pond and this tree," he will wonder. "They look just like the pond and tree I spent my youth playing with." Memories will flood back to him. He will scoop the pond water into his hands, feel the rough bark of the tree and then his instincts will urge him - as all humans are the same with memories of old - they will urge him to climb the tree. Once up, balanced on a branch the second part of the plan will slither into action."

"It best be better than the first part." The Devil giving up all hope, couldn't even muster up the energy to shut the dweeb up.

"I promise sire, I will not fail you. There will be a snake."

"Oh of course, now there's a bloody snake. First an apple and now a snake. Hurry up!"

"The snake will slither silently up to Zed and hiss: "Hello Zed". This no doubt will startle him, you see humans are not used to talking snakes."

The Devil slapped his head in animated sarcastic shock.

"The snake will go on to explain how a bite of the one red apple in the tree will bring all that he has ever desired to be his for eternity. A human cannot resist a snake promising everything from a bite of a sweet red apple."

A bit more intrigued the Devil gestured with his hand to carry on.

"One bite of the only red apple in the tree will not give him pleasure. It will in fact turn him to stone. At which point, one of your demons can pick him up and bring him down here. We would have used temptation to trick him - which I believe is God's least favourite vice. The stone statue can be left as a reminder to God of how powerful we are and you would have Zed." Seeing the Devil needed just one more nibble to win him over he continued. "On the stone statue we will engrave 'Banished from the Garden of Zed by the Dark Lord'."

"Fucking genius." The Devil stood up smiling, almost hugging this plan-making dweeb to bursting point. He would enjoy watching this.

The tension in the room subsided as the Devil left. "But your plan is stolen from a book. I plagiarised mine and he went mad," moaned a fellow project manager.

"Yes but I chose a book he has never read."

"They say the Devil has read all books that have ever been written."

"Yes, but he refuses to read the bible out of principle. He says it portrays him in a unfair light."

"Seems pretty accurate to me!"

The general murmur around the room certainly had the air of consensus.

Chapter Twenty Nine

To Zed's great relief there was only a quick walk to a taxi. Waiting patiently he noticed a group of men running around the corner. Back and forth they were running yet always coming closer. He saw a carriage speeding along behind them but couldn't see anything pulling it. "Must be engine powered, but I thought they were banned." As it got closer, things clicked and he saw what it was. "Of course, logs. Everything is powered by rolling logs. Even taxis," he said out loud.

Ten minutes later and they were zooming along in a comfy carriage. "Let me get this two hundred percent clear. You fellas move everything with logs?"

"Yes, sir."

"Even small things like chairs?"

"It's more efficient, sir."

"No it's not you blithering imbecile," Zed thought watching the two guys on this log powered taxi frantically running from back to front, moving the logs while another two pushed. Really you'd have imagined that they were sick of this whole transporting objects via logs, but once in heaven old traditions are hard to break.

"Here you are, sir and madam."

"Thanks and cheerio."

Standing imposingly in front of them was a gigantic pyramid. Not like the large ones on earth, more a colossal sized, mega pyramid. What you have to remember is that in heaven time is on your side and you have plenty of it to concentrate on your hobby. When the best pyramid builders that ever lived had eternity to kill, they went to town on their pyramids.

"Mighty impressive. But I will not have time to go round the whole thing as I must be getting back to the donkey train to catch the next one back to my home."

"Home? Home is with family, I always think myself," said his guide.

Zed mumbled something in forced agreement. He also noticed a slight wind gently blowing some sand around his feet. Strange he thought: "I've not noticed any wind before."

"Shall we start? This is the pyramid of Tutankhamen's chief slave. Built by ten thousand lesser slaves, and with a construction time of eight hundred years to complete. All the slaves - oops, sorry, slip of the tongue - I mean workmen loved every day on site. Mainly down to whipping being banned."

"But why would they do it when they can relax and enjoy heaven?"

"It's in their blood. Hard workers, Egyptians love the sense of achievement. As soon as this one was built we were on to the next one; always bigger than the last, as well. Try telling a Egyptian that bigger isn't always best."

All around the entrance of the largest pyramid to ever exist, elegantly carved pictures were brought to life with bright colours, contrasting against the sandy colour of the stones used to build the walls."

"After you, Zed."

So Zed did as he was told and walked through the huge entrance, his hands in pockets, concentrating on nothing and feeling gloomy.

Swoosh, swoosh.

"Ahhhh I've been killed!"

"Ha ha ha. Calm down."

"I've been sliced in half. Well I must have been."

A giant axe swung across Zed's path as he entered the pyramid, and then swung right back missing him by inches.

"You're still all in one piece, Zed. It was just a booby trap," the guide giggled behind her hand.

Wiping a few sweat drops from his brow with a shaky hand, Zed conducted some slow breathing exercises and recovered composure. "This is heaven. I thought things like this were banned?"

"You can't have an Egyptian pyramid without booby traps. But as it's in heaven none of them should actually hurt you. They may scare you, but that's part of the fun on my tour."

"Mightily mean I'd say putting old me through that without warning. I'd like to point out I am not comfortable with your use of 'should' or 'fun'. That was not in my definition of fun and 'should' has an ambiguous feel to instead of a statement of fact."

"I'm sorry sir, just a joke."

"No more jokes please."

"Yes, your wish is my command. Let's go forth."

Inside it struck Zed how many Egyptian artefacts filled the room. Squeezed into any available space stood statues, vases, rugs, replica mini pyramids, Sphinxes and more.

Ahead of them were two separate paths to take. One ramp going up and one going down.

"Good planning," thought Zed. "Makes this pyramid wheelchair friendly."

A handy signpost explained your choices. The pointing down arrow had a remarkably amateurish picture of a gold coffin, while the up arrow had a picture of a pit with snakes in.

"Which way first Zed?"

"Well in all honesty I only have time for one, so let's avoid the snake pit. Sounds more hell than heaven to me."

"Oh well, if you insist."

She said that in a very mischievous way Zed thought.

Always so gullible, humans. History teachers and films directors alike have attempted to drum into our brains that pyramids are booby trapped. When in a place built to trick and deceive, in its attempt to fend you off the treasure that lurks within, then a good bit of advice is to ignore helpfully placed signposts. Luckily for Zed, he could not die at the hands of a well-placed trap. To die, when one has already died, is a concept that can be deadly in itself, if too much thought is put into the idea. For thousands of years the greats of Greece spent their lives working on this, coming to the only logical conclusion that everyone agreed upon. They declared that to die while already dead was in fact very, very, very bad luck.

Following this peculiar woman, Zed couldn't help looking at the large lumps she possessed on her back. Brought up to know it's rude to stare, he tried desperately to avert his attention somewhere else but his eyes kept being drawn back and his brain kept hammering on his head that he had met this woman before.

"And here you can see where the wall has been carved to show the faces of his entire family ..." She was doing her best to put on a good tour but Zed heard no history. Each word sounded like his dad hated him and his mum wanted to never see him again.

"Is it almost finished? As I'm sure I saw that the next train departed soon."

"Yes if you just step through here, we are pretty much at the end."

"Ok." Zed stepped through.

THUD.

The earth shook; dust filled the air, chunks of the walls crumbled, falling to the floor. The ground wobbled for what felt like eternity, the whole room was now filled with dust causing Zed's lungs to cough up half the desert he had swallowed over the last few days.

"I can't die, I can't die," Zed's brain drummed out his new mantra on overdrive.

Eventually after the longest twenty seconds in Zed's record books, the shaking ceased and Zed pulled himself up off the ground he had found himself flat on.

"Hello, I think I'm alive, are you there?"

Groping the air, Zed's sleuth detective hands fondled a wall made of large boulders that a minute prior did not exist. Realising he was now separated from the annoying woman, which ironically was annoying in itself.

"Yes, yes. I'm so sorry Zed. It appears a new booby trap has been put in that I knew nothing about. If you just follow the passage round and take your next right you will be at the exit and I'll meet you there."

"Oh righto."

Feeling angry that this stupid guide had made him go on a ridiculously dangerous tour of which he had no interest, he muttered some unthinkables under his breath. And then his brain kicked in.

"I could power walk, get out before she gets there and make my escape."

The dust had cleared to reveal a long path curving round to the right. All the brightly coloured carvings now had the appearance of dusty untouched artefacts. Giving a few brief moments of interest to the boulders that had fallen so perfectly to form an impenetrable wall, and then off Zed walked. Bum wiggling from side to side trying to get the maximum speed without breaking into an unthinkable run.

"Why did I agree to go on this tour?" he moaned to himself. "I agreed to walk, which I hate, around a pyramid, which I now loath."

Picking up speed no other walker had yet achieved, he rounded a tight bend and froze. His ears pricked up like an Egyptian sphinx on the hunt. In the distance, or very close there could be heard a murmur. Like someone was trapped underground, maybe in pain. "Ah, just more tourists I guess, their guide sounds worse than mine," he thought allowing his body to relax. Off his legs went, lifting his left foot high off the ground to gain maximum speed ready for the right to follow.

Tap, tap went a yet unidentified object on his shoulder.

"Ah people at last," he thought spinning round, hand stretched out, anticipating a heart warming handshake, Zed turned to greet these tourists.

This time he froze solid, then thawed like an ice cream licked by a hungry volcano.

"Ahhhhh!" he screamed and made a dash for a sharp exit.

His legs rotated like a tuned racing car's pistons. They took longer than normal, due to current circumstances, to relay a message back to the brain that he wasn't moving, despite his seemingly speedy get away. At lightning speed, a soft small powerful hand had reached out and grabbed him by the shoulders, lifting him a foot off the ground.

"Let me go, let me go, please let me go."

"You have come into my sacred pyramid and disturbed the great ascent into our promised Kingdom!" the owner of the powerful hand bellowed, words vibrating off all walls.

"But you're already in heaven, there is no promised Kingdom beyond what is essentially the promised Kingdom," Zed protested.

The fear paralysing his vision had started to allow Zed to look at his captor and question why it was wrapped head to toe in white linen. All that you could see were two eyes.

"A mummy! It's a bloody mummy and it talks! How do you escape a mummy? Silver? No that was for werewolves. Stake? Punch them in the eye? Why do history teachers never teach the important stuff?" Feeling the need to escape urgently, Zed played dirty.

"Awww!" the mummy whined. A kick as hard as possible worked wonders. The mummy released its grip and Zed wasted no time in making his escape. Risking a quick glance over his shoulder as he ran, he heard the mummy shout a blood curdling sentence. "You can escape my grip, but you cannot escape my curse. For this life and beyond you are cursed for eternity."

He could hear the mummy getting closer and closer and fear drenched his body that had a good coating of exercise sweat already. Faster! his brain commanded, faster!

Chapter Thirty

If you happened to achieve the impossible and view heaven in its entirety from above, which of course only One has ever done before, you'd start to notice the winds around the edges, slowly and discreetly as possible, gathering together. "Nothing to see here," the wind would say to any onlookers as it formed gangs, which then absorbed other gangs. They were starting to circle around the edges of heaven and were always growing. It wasn't a violent or vicious get together, just a steady stream of winds accumulating - angry, very angry winds at that.

Chapter Thirty One

Right in the centre of heaven - if mathematically it were possible to define something that doesn't logically have a centre - was a small cottage of no distinct features to note. The couple living there kept themselves to themselves and enjoyed a simple life of pottering around their garden, with occasional breaks for food, drink and sleep. If they had any spare time they could be found tending to one of their four allotment plots. When first constructed, the heavenly house builders had questioned the wisdom of having to go to four allotments when they could have just built a larger garden instead, but they had come to understand that almost all humans, if being polite, were a bit weird and, if being honest, were stupid. On this beautiful morning, Cath was up early checking for slugs as she did every day. Proof, the builders would declare, of the 'humans being stupid' argument, as all slugs go to hell. The occasional brightly coloured snail gets in through heaven's gates but has to sign a stack of papers promising not to ruin the common gardeners' plants. Pete walked out with two large coffees and called over to Cath to take a rest. Sipping their coffees and enjoying heavenly life, a visitor arrived.

"Hello, fellow heaven people. I am here to check your gas."

"No need sir, we do not have gas," replied Pete

"Not gas? I meant electricity?"

"Nope, none of that either. Goodbye."

"Er, er. Well can I just check your house to make sure?"

"No, that won't be required. I'm an expert at spotting gas and electricity and have found none in my home since we moved to heaven. Good day and good bye."

The guy shuffled off muttering something under his breath.

"Yet another one dear," said Pete.

"Yes dear. Wonder where they come from?"

For the last few days a stranger would turn up trying to look at something they did not have in their home. Not to worry they thought, as there is never anything to worry about in heaven.

The guy who did have to worry was making his way as slowly as demonly possible back to hell wondering what Satan would do to him for failing to scout out Zed's parents home. The demon that failed the day before was slowly being melted into glue. The Devil had broken his favourite vase and nothing sticks like demon glue.

Chapter Thirty Two

Puffing and panting, Zed burst out of the entrance and ran straight into a rudely placed solid wall. Waking up a few moments later with birds swirling round his head he screamed. Half of Egypt heard his scream. It took him a few seconds to remember why he was screaming, but as soon as he did, his legs were trying to get him to bolt off further away from that mummy.

"Hey Zed, found your way out?"

It was the woman guide.

"A mummy! there was a mummy!"

"You want your mummy?"

"No there was a bloody mummy in there and it cursed me and tried to kill me. Why are you hobbling, did you hurt yourself?"

"No someone hurt me," she mumbled under her breath. "You don't need to worry about that mummy. You know you can't be killed in heaven."

Some of the dread dried up on Zed's body. "So the curse wasn't true either?"

"No, the curse is true."

"That's good. Hold on - it is true? So I am cursed? But no, that's terrible."

"It's just a curse. Calm down. We Egyptians suffered lashing thirty hours a day and, if we refused to work, had our brains pulled through our noses. We would love to have been cursed instead. You don't know the meaning of hardship."

"I don't want to be cursed though," Zed said in a pleading, defeated sort of way.

"Then go find your parents," the guide said as casually as she could.

"Well, I was going to. Hang on what do you mean 'go find my parents'? What's that got to do with the curse? Stick to the curse please. It's frightfully worrying and I don't want to see my parents thank you very much."

"Why don't you want to see your parents, Zed? I reckon they will be missing you."

"No they are not and I asked you nicely to stick to the curse." Zed was turning red in anger.

"I am sticking to the curse. Do you not know about breaking a curse?"

"No. Surprisingly, we didn't have any lessons in breaking curses."

"Schools these days - pathetic. Well a curse like this one can only be broken by the hug of your parents. Nice and simple. Like a prince frog needs a princess to kiss him."

"Now you're blathering on about frogs, stick to the curse." Zed was getting exasperated.

"Calm down and listen. To break the curse, just hug your parents. It's written on the walls of the pyramid."

Bemused Zed sought clarification. "Let me get this straight. I just need to hug my parents and then I am de-cursed? The curse is gone, banished to curse hell?"

"That summarises what I have just said, yes."

Zed thought about his two options. Go home to his bar but be cursed for eternity. Or carry on and force a hug from his unloving parents who did not want to see him, let alone embrace their cursed son.

"Well I suppose I can go and see them. " The words coming out were covered in a bitter taste. "I mean, I don't have to stay."

But Zed was talking to himself. The woman had vanished into thin air. Although in heaven the air is actually thick.

High above Zed, the Angel Elemiah smiled. I knew I could trick him. Best return this mummy costume before the shop closes, she thought.

Zed meanwhile cursed the cursed curse.

Chapter Thirty Three

"Over the many years you have known me, all here will have observed that I have the patience of a saint. Yet this past week, I've been tested. Because you little fuckers can't do anything right! If I said jump you'd sit and if I said sit you'd jump. My patience has run out. You," the Devil singled out a soon to be doomed demon, "why did a demon of your calibre fail to enter the house of Zed's parents? All you have to do is install a simple hell door for convenient access to their home from hell. But no, it seems the two old people managed to fight you off. Did they attack you?"

"No," the demon said with a commendable amount of confidence for one who knew this conversation was only going to get worse.

"Did they have impenetrable walls surrounding their home?"

"No," was the slightly less confident and a lot quieter reply.

"Shark-tipped, nuclear weapon defence system?"

"Er no. Not that I saw. They did have a fish pond though."

"Shut it!"

"Sorry me Lord, just when you mentioned sharks I suddenly remembered the fish pond. And your suggestion made me think that perhaps they did have some sort of shark related defence system." (A desperate last attempt to avoid the inevitable.)

The Devil looked at his demon in bemused anger and ignored his last stupid comment.

"So what may I ask, stopped a demon of your calibre in your mission?"

"They had no gas," the demon felt in safer ground here.

"No gas?"

"Or electricity."

The Devil's horns normally the colour of night had a hint of red, and steam seemed to be shooting out from their tips.

"And what the fuck does no gas or electricity have anything to do with this?"

"Well your sire, I was cunningly disguised as the gas man?"

"Gas man?!"

"Yes, the gas man."

"Gas man?'"

"Yes." Thinking the Devil was struggling to hear, the demon repeated very slowly and loudly: "Gas man."

Other bystanders in the room took cover, an exploding volcano can cause some damage but no one has witnessed what an exploding Devil can do.

"I heard you the first time!"

"Well, when they said no gas or electricity my cover was blown."

The demon had now seen his once promising explanation would not please his master.

"My arse could have still worked out a way to get in, you bullshit excuse for a demon. Bring in the hedgehogs. I'm going to show you what happens to all who fail me!"

Fear made its evil dance across the demon's face. "No! Not the hedgehogs!"

Chapter Thirty Four

Hovering high above, Elemiah watched Zed for a while. Humans fascinated her. The way they can be extremely gullible and dumb, yet have created such wonders on earth. Half daydreaming and half observing Zed, it took her senses a while to notice the wind. Earlier in the day she had felt the breeze at ground level and thought it odd. Even a slight gust was unheard of in heaven, yet up where she was now the air put up a good fight, trying to unsteady her normally effortless hover. In the far off distance she could just make out clouds slowly forming. Not storm clouds, just regular white fluffy clouds. "Oh crap," she thought and flew off at the speed of an Angel, which is slower than light but faster than a tortoise.

Zed meanwhile was pounding the sandy floor back and forth. He'd pounded it for some time and there was now quite a deep channel dug into the sand along the line he'd walked. If Zed carried on like this he would have found himself walking in hell.

"On the one hand, I can go and force a hug off my parents, then make the long journey back to my bar. Or I go straight back and risk this curse being real. Damn it! Why did my expensive, private school education not prepare me for this?"

What was needed was a stiff drink. "Excuse me," he said to a passing guy who was log rolling his shopping home, "is there a bar around theses parts?"

It took Zed half an hour to find the bar that was two minutes from where he started. Ever since directions were first given out to a passing stranger they have always been incorrect or confusing. No logical explanation has ever been found to explain this strange, unintended behaviour. Some experts in this field of study have muted the possibility that brains secretly revel in giving out dodgy directions knowing that the asker's brain has to follow the bad instructions.

Sitting down at the bar, Zed waited to be served. If you were led into this public house blindfolded and had no idea where in heaven you were, then the ancient Egyptian zone would not be your first guess. The bar was not what you'd expect from people who lived in the time of the Pharaohs. For a start it had a pinball machine and a jukebox.

"Gidday, mate. What can I get ya? Got some tinnies cooling out back." A cheery sort of chap appeared from behind the bar.

"I would love a gin and tonic please, if you have one."

Selecting a glass and pouring the drink expertly, the barman looked Zed up and down. "Say, you're not from round these parts are yah?"

"No, I'm just passing through."

Like all good landlords the Australian sounding chap effortlessly flowed into a quick story about himself, so as to get acquainted. "Ha. That's what I said ten years ago. The name's Fredo. Nice to meet yah. I had got bored where I was in heaven. My neighbours, Sheilas, the both of them, were goody two shoes and wouldn't shut up about how great God is. I mean, sure he made us this heaven and all, but no need to go on about it. So I decided to go on a whopper of an adventure. It's what I did on earth, so why not do it in heaven? This was a detour from my planned destination. I was heading to the great, unexplored jungles, where no human has ever been or been found. But when I came here I thought, wowzer what a great place this is to rest for a bit. Plenty to explore and do. Somehow I've ended up staying ever since. Great people the Egyptians. Love a dance and a practical joke."

Zed was intrigued. "Will you stay here forever?"

"Doubt it. As soon as I get bored I'll up and off again. Here's yah drink. Enjoy."

Taking a swift sip of his drink before carrying on he asked: "Is there a map round here? See I'm off to find my parents."

His lips moved before his brain had chance to think.

"Well, I mean I was off to find them but now I may not be," Zed tried backtracking from his un-thought out statement.

"Why the change of heart mate? Sounds like your brain's as confused as a prawn thrown on the barbie."

"Just certain feelings telling me they don't want to see me?"

"Well, I'm not going to tell him I saw my future. I've no intention of coming across like a madman," Zed thought.

"A feeling? I once had a feeling I was the reincarnation of Sir Ralph Reynolds. After meeting him up here once it turns out I was wrong. Good idea that about seeing your family. Makes me want to go and see mine now."

The barman was cleaning a glass and had the look of deep concentration, no doubt flicking through some forgotten memories of good times with his own flesh and blood. Or maybe just baby 'roos - either thought is enough to put a smile on anyone's lips.

"Sorry to disturb your concentration, but a map? Do you know where one is?"

"Hold on a sec."

He dashed off into the back of the bar and returned a few moments later with some rolled up, old looking, brown paper.

"I got these from an Angel. Bet him he couldn't lift a chair up one handed by the bottom of one leg. I won."

He rolled out an intricately decorated map of heaven that stretched the length of the bar. The map, unknown to the barman, was one of the oldest items in heaven. The Angel he'd cunningly acquired the map from feared everyday that someone would discover that he had lost the great map of Hiyahichi made from ancient palaerious trees, mulched into thick, unbreakable paper and decorated by the cherub himself. Entrusted to look after this one-off irreplaceable item, he would not be looked kindly upon for losing it. One day he will be audited and the loss shall be discovered. He prays the punishment uses no sentence with the word 'hell' in it.

"See here, that's where we are now. Where is it you need to get to?"

"The twentieth century zone," Zed said without thinking.

"Seems you've made up my mind again brain," he thought. "Not sure you consulted me fully on this one."

"That, Pommie, would take years to get to."

"Oh well, I could just go home I suppose."

"Don't be a failure mate. You cut through here and then you could be there within a few days."

Not sure whether to be happy or annoyed, Zed mumbled something in agreement.

"Why did you say it would take several years but now you have magically changed your time estimate to a few days?"

"Well on the map these things are hard to see. Throughout heaven there are several, so called, 'snail holes' that can be used as shortcuts. No one is sure whether God intentionally created them or if they are a mistake, but for us travellers they're handy to know about."

Zed remembered the map man mentioning them but, having followed his directions up to this point, he needed reminding on the remainder of his journey.

"Guess I'm off to find my parents then. Damn this curse."

"Sorry what curse?"

"Curse? Oh you must have misheard I said..." Zed tried desperately to think of a word that rhymed or sounded like curse and ended up with "purse."

"Damn your purse?"

"Yes it's um, well you see." Giving up Zed stood up and said: "Nice meeting you. Thanks for the advice. Must be going now. Bye."

And with that he was gone.

Chapter Thirty Five

To experience twenty straight hours of torture with hedgehogs dished out by the Devil sounds like hell. And it was. Some hell dwellers see it as an honour to be tortured by the boss, proving that some people are dim bats. Watching the demon being dragged out, looking bewildered and traumatised, by his feet covered in hedgehog spines, the Devil chuckled. When it was first suggested as a torture method he ridiculed the idea; now it was one of his best-loved techniques.

Even so, he was in no mood to enjoy himself and for the last hour of torture Satan let the hedgehogs do their bidding and had taken a back seat. He needed to ruminate. Shaking off the urge to sleep, he grabbed a tannoy horn and spoke in his formal business voice.

"Cough, cough. Attention Agares, Baphomet, Crocell and Demogorgen. Report to the Honey Badger meeting room now. Any late arrivals will be punished unconditionally with a trip to Skegness."

Five minutes later the meeting was starting, no one had dared be late.

The torture session coupled with the stress of Zed had taken its toll on the Devil. With two matches literally holding his eyes open and dreaming of sleep, he got straight to the point. "All four of you will be going to heaven immediately after this meeting. Your trip will be simple. Go to Zed's parents' house, enter Zed's fucking parents' house and open a goddamn door to hell." Tiredness had affected his normal meeting manner and profanities poured out from his mouth. "No fucking failures this time. Use whatever means you want. Fucking walk up, knock them out and tie them up in their bedroom. Do whatever is needed. I don't give a shit how you get the job done as long as you lot don't fuck up. Just don't let anyone see ok! We need to keep heaven's attention off them for now. You, with your hand up, it best be a good question else the hand will get a choppy choppy."

"Yes sorry er I mean er.."

"Hurry up you ass, the knifey knifey is on its way to your hand."

"Just, well can you confirm? We can use force?"

The Devil was silent. Bed was what he craved not some idiotic question from a so-called demon.

"Did you, as a demon, the embodiment of pure evil, just ask if you could use force?"

"Well we will be in heaven. We don't want to annoy you know who."

The Devil's eyes glowed with absolute rage but his voice kept calm.

"Annoy who?"

"No one, sir."

Seeing he had rattled the demon he teased him more. "Oh, Mr No One from Notown in Noville?"

"Yes that's him," the demon squirmed in panic mode.

"You're scared of God, ain't you? Look at you all. Pathetic frightened dip shits the lot of you. I'm the fucking boss. You understand? I'm the one to be scared of. What's he going to do? Tickle you?"

Another of the demons made the mistake of suggesting a few options. "He could drown us, or make us kill our son or send a plague of evil stuff."

"Shut up, shut up. When I'm in charge up there as well as down here, things will change! There will only be one to fear and obey. Now get the fuck out here and do my bidding!"

"Yes, your Grace", and they hurried off.

Collapsing head first into the table out of frustration and exhaustion, Satan would have wept if it were possible. Mustering up the energy he stood up, stared briefly at the Devil face shaped hole in the solid iron table, turned and went to find his bed.

Chapter Thirty Six

It may flabbergast many to discover that since man was created there have been cults and people willing to join them. One quarter of humans are born with this fault.

After escaping a crucifixion, ruining a football match and gaining a sizeable amount of new followers in Roman times, Bob resumed his ministry. Playing it by ear and following his nose, he'd found himself in the 'so-called' caveman zone. Soon Bob wished he had followed his eyes rather than his ears or nose. You see (as Bob clearly didn't) cavemen like big clubs. What they especially like is clubbing things with their big clubs.

After numerous clubbings by several cavemen, Bob picked up the basics of their language. A language with one word - or more accurately one sound - "grunt", that had the possibility of meaning anything. A few grunts later and Bob had escaped his club beaters with his newly learned, wondrous sound. Admiring crowds circled round him, dazzled by the crude pictures of Zed drawn by Bob on a cave wall. Leaving soon after, he had identified the humans with the gullible fault, and was leading them away to search for more followers. It felt good and Bob wanted more, much more.

Chapter Thirty Seven

Tending to her favourite rhododendron, Cath felt like she was in heaven. In a few seconds Pete, her darling husband, would be bringing out a summer cocktail which they'd enjoy drinking slowly on their garden bench. Kneeling down on her soft gardening kneepad she checked for weeds, and as per every time she checked, none were found. Happy that her flowerbed was weeded, pruned and watered she got to her feet. Pete arrived with drinks and they sat down hand in hand enjoying death.

Approaching their house they could see a group of men briskly marching towards their front gate.

"Oh dear, here comes some more people. Go tell them we do not have gas or electricity before they trample on our lawn."

Pete, drink in hand, plodded slowly down to their gate to meet the men.

"Excuse me gentlemen, but we don't have gas or electricity and have no need for insulation and never buy things from door to door salesmen."

"Well it's your lucky day then isn't it," Baphomet replied grinning.

"Why?"

"As we just want to tie you up."

"No, we don't want that either. Sorry, did you say 'tie us up'?"

Acting out their master's wishes, the demons did not pussy foot around and made their move. Baphomet and Demogorgen grabbed Pete while the other two bolted the gate and restrained Cath before she had a chance to scream. Being elderly, they didn't put up much of a struggle and soon had been dragged inside. They lay silent on their living room floor, gagged, bound and terrified.

Highly pleased with their work so far, the demons celebrated with some general abusive language. "Good job you stinking bunch of cocks. Now where shall we install the door to hell?"

Agares felt he was best qualified to answer this owing to his recent course undertaken on the very subject. "The toilet obviously." Quoting from his lecturer, he carried on: "When installing a door to hell you should consider ease of access and, just as importantly, the dramatic and overall effect any entrance may have."

The other demons looked quite impressed so he continued.

"Imagine a human seeing a demon rise from the bowels of hell. Rising through a toilet would be perfect; any human watching would crap himself."

This was agreed upon by the four demons and the building of the door commenced. To build a door to hell does not require bricks and mortar. First you need a demon or an equivalent evil being. Secondly you need the chosen evil one to chant the chant of the Devil. The sound created is similar to an angry cat – one that had mutated into a stegosaurus sized cat and grown a much deeper voice - fighting for his territory. It's not a nice sound and most guidebooks would suggest avoiding viewing or hearing the ritual.

All four of the demons went upstairs to find the bathroom and located a lovely, white, clean toilet ideal for their use.

Crocell begged to be allowed to perform the chant, as he had never opened a hell door before. The others, being veterans on hell doors, gladly allowed him as they were all well aware of how boring and tiring it can be.

Watching Crocell struggle to keep it up, Demogorgen brought up an earlier discussion they had about how to gain entrance to Zed's parents home.

"I still think we should have pretended to be conservatory salesmen."

Chapter Thirty Eight

Easing back into his shiny red leather Chesterfield sofa, a gut wrenching sound of evil bones creaking and joints cracking was emitted from the Devil's tired body. Stress over the millennia had aged and perished the Devil's already ravaged frame. Thousands of years living in a volcanic environment wore heavily on his wrinkled face. Where once there was muscle, now lay fat. How come all masseurs get into heaven he always wondered? He craved a good massage. All he had down in hell were a bunch of chiropractors. Ironically they aimed to fix crooked backs, yet they are all a bunch of crooks themselves. After allowing these con artists to fix his ravaged spine, he realised why they all ended up in hell. Few have made the Devil scream but they managed it. Feeling a thousand times worse, they assured him his back would get better with more treatment. Five sessions later and the Devil had had enough. Pleasingly he came up with a well-suited torture regime for them. A simple rota had been drawn up to allow them to practise on each other. The screams emitted from the sessions brought tears of joy to Satan's eyes.

Five minutes of relaxing and the Devil was ready to think about work again. Precisely drawn on his new white board, purchased after reading about them in 'Evil Plans for Dummies', lay his three-pronged plan in action. Hearing just now, and to his great surprise, of the successful installation and opening of his requested hell door at Zed's parents' house, he reached out and ticked action one as complete. Action two, highlighted in red, was to cause maximum attention when using trap, followed by the words 'Top Secret'. Lastly, in capitals he'd written 'GREAT WALL'. For the Devil knew if Zed was to reach his parents quickly, then there was only one route - he must go through the snail hole.

The plan, just like so many of his most stupid plans, came to him in a dream. Waking up in a state of excitement, he reached for his bedside horn to summon the project planners to an instant meeting. He explained the cunningness of the plan to the attendees in the meeting; they had all had tried their best to show enthusiasm, and so after an hour the great 'Great Wall' of the snail hole project was formed. In basic terms, all the thousands of cowboy builders wasting away in hell were rounded up and ushered off and up to heaven for the building of an impenetrable wall, stretching the whole breadth of the snail hole.

Reading the three-point plan again brought comfort to his tortured soul, (although the Devil didn't have a soul). He felt the stress ooze from his body as he studied the whiteboard, happy in the knowledge that all was finally going to plan.

Chapter Thirty Nine

Lurking in the shadows of shadows, where only the unseen horrors go to hide, was a Thing. An indescribable Thing. If you wanted condensed purified evil then this was it. Not evil that can be mastered over a lifetime; more if something is born with one purpose - of being evil. Skilfully avoiding any detection, darting from corner to corner few ever got to see it. The unlucky minority that did see looked away and tried to forget.

Spotting today's prey, its mouth hung open, foaming with evil excitement. If it possessed a heart, the beat would be racing as though nitrous oxide was supercharging the heart. Nothing got the Thing more on edge and excited as the chase.

In heaven there are good people and Angels, and in hell there were the damned and demons. Of course, some people are lost in purgatory. And then there are Things. Not created by God but the creation of dreams. Hanging in limbo, the dream world skirts both heaven and hell. Physically and mathematically impossible to exist, yet still there.

Humans love to sleep. The laziest ones would never wake up if they had their way. Drifting asleep they are unaware of the dangers that await. Some of the most annoying humans will wake and recite their dreams to others, always convinced the dream is a prediction or suggestion of the future. They are wrong. It's more likely to be a failed attempt at assassinating the sleeper. Terrifyingly, sometimes a dream becomes so real it can escape. This particular despicable Thing was the dream, or nightmare, of a child called Rosie. Ever since her nightmare the girl's parents had endured sleepless nights, waking every few hours to witness Rosie climbing into their bed, squeezing between Mum and Dad and screaming the house down, too scared to return to her monster-infested room.

Escaped Things discovered their unique talent and cornered a niche job market down in hell - bounty hunting. This Thing had its bounty in site. Zed, having just left the bar had a spring in his step.

The Thing smiled to itself: "I'll turn that spring into frozen winter soon."

The Devil had put a contract on Zed's head - just as a backup backup-plan. The reward was his body. He had the power to give these disgusting Things a human form, and they would do anything for it. All the 'wanted' poster said was, 'Bring Zed to Hell'. The Thing had not thought about how he would transport Zed to hell but knew how to catch him.

Zed found himself walking through a dark street but in heaven dark streets did not pose a danger. People walk about with not a care or thought of danger. The sound of rapid gun fire, followed by screams and a explosion thrown in for good measure, would produce very little reaction from anyone that heard. A simple shrug of their shoulders and a "must be just some kids playing" is about as much as you'd get. People feel safe in heaven.

The Thing was close behind and getting closer. Each step Zed took the Thing edged nearer. The stench of the Thing grew worse as it approached, and Zed was sure the sky was getting darker. And then the Thing went to pounce. "Good day," Zed said to a passing couple. The Thing had squirmed into a hole in the road to hide from the people. The Devil hated others knowing bad events are happening in heaven, so it knew there would be no reward if anyone saw him. The couple passed and off the Thing went - hunting, quickly catching up with Zed again. This time it found Zed walking through a small wooded area and appeared well hidden by trees. The stench now in the air made Zed stop. Ready to pounce, the Thing looked like an alligator stalking its next baby wildebeest. Zed started walking again faster now to escape the smell, and then the Thing attacked.

Chapter Forty

Elemiah, against her better judgement, sat tapping her fingers rhythmically on a table waiting for everyone to turn up to her meeting. Angels hate meetings so she expected, at most, half the invited to be present, and almost all of them late. In general, Angels are more your hippy, dope smoking, save the whale types, rather than suit wearing meeting lovers.

Only ten Angels currently sat around the table out of an invited fifty. She knew a few more would turn up soon tempted by the tea and biscuits promised in the invitation, but how many she could not say.

They were not so much in a room but in the sky. Being highly suspicious of humans eavesdropping on important Angel business, all meetings took place where humans could not go. There's an issue with this; it's a feature found with all tables and understood by all - tables cannot fly. To rectify this commonly overlooked defect required four less senior Angels, some rope and knots. Tying a rope around each table leg, the four angles would lift the table up into the sky and were expected to hover for the entire meeting. Then there are chairs. Rope must be wrapped around both chair and Angel, whose backside would be seated on said chair so they could hover high in the sky while seated. Many a human has laughed watching this ridiculous practice, but the Angels are unaware of any ridicule, always assuming they were idolised by the inferior human race. Sitting up high, they felt mightily important and certainly never stupid.

"Right, let's get started," Elemiah shouted above the noise of beating wings and raised voices.

"When's the tea coming?" voiced a concerned Angel.

"Yes, good point, and not forgetting the biscuits," another agreed.

"Soon, I promise," she lied. "Now I've brought you all together today to discuss my unusual observations over the last few days. A new heavener, by the name of Zed, seems to have caused some unwanted activity from down below."

Rudely interrupting in an un-angelic way, an Angel shouted out: "Is he someone special on earth. One of these celebrities or footballers?"

"No. Well, not that I know. I think he was just your regular sort off plonker, standard human breed. Nice guy though."

"Who cares then?" They were rapidly losing interest.

"The Devil," Elemiah announced in her most dramatic voice.

Expecting uproar, excitement or something, she felt taken aback by the muted reaction she received. Attempting again with even more drama resonating from her vocal chords: "I said the Devil, Satan, the antichrist!"

"So what. He's down in hell. You know the big man always deals with him if he tries anything."

"But this time it feels different. This guy is a nobody, someone who has gone unnoticed down on earth and in all plausible theories should continue causing less ripples in our kingdom of heaven. Well how come then he has so far fought off Dantalion, Xaphan, Corson and Botis in the few days the guy's been here?"

This last comment had the desired effect and upped the excitement in the room - or floating open office.

"He repelled attacks by all these demons? Is he a trained fighter?"

Another Angel joined in. "Did you witness this attack, and he fought them off all at the same time?"

"The Otis? No human could stop the Otis," shouted a third Angel.

Knowing she would have to come clean she answered in a more muffled voice than before: "Not all at once, more one at a time."

"Still," the most impressed Angel said, "it's jolly good going for a human to defend himself from one demon, let alone four separate attacks. What form of defence did he use?"

Taking a deep intake of breath, Elemiah confessed: "None really. He sort of just didn't notice them and things sorted themselves out."

Great laughter erupted around the table and Elemiah turned a nice shade of anger. "Listen you low life excuse for Angels. Something is going on. Zed turned up at my hotel convinced, for no apparent reason, he needed to see his parents. Ever since, demons have been popping up doing there best to stop him. I don't know why but we must all help Zed find his parents. The future of heaven is at stake."

The fury emitted from her voice silenced the table, yet one of the less clever Angels continued to snigger.

"You snigger all you like, but when God finds out you are prepared to risk heaven and all that we believe in, then God help you that he doesn't do what he once did to Lucifer."

Angels twiddled their thumbs, looked down at the table and perspired slightly. One subject that was always ignored, never spoken about, and certainly never used as a threat, is that of Lucifer.

Seraphim, feeling she should do something being the senior Angel broke the silence.

"You had better be proved right about this. Bringing up the unspeakable is no laughing matter and there will be dire consequences for you if you're making this up."

"Honestly, there are strange things afoot. Have you noticed the wind?"

Around the table Angels nodded. Each having noticed the wind and almost instantly attempting to un-notice it in case they had to do something about it.

Seraphim, regretting her intervention, felt she had no choice but to carry on. "Yes, admittedly that is strange. It seems to be getting stronger each day. And I swear I saw a grey cloud. What of it though?"

Knowing everyone was now paying attention, Elemiah felt more in control. "I think Zed, the Devil and the wind are all related. For me, it can only mean one thing and that is Satan has a plan and we need to guarantee Zed is reunited with his parents to foil this evil plan. Together we Angels are strong. We can defeat Satan if we all stick together. Who's with me?" She roared.

Popping her confidence balloon with silence, the Angels appeared less excited or committed to helping Zed than she'd hoped for. At last someone spoke.

"Will there be tea?"

"Oh for fuck sake, come on, feel the wind, feel the danger. Just like the old days, we can stand together against evil."

"But will there be tea, there was always tea in the old days?" Everyone agreed full heartedly that in the old days they were never short on tea.

"Oh alright, there will be tea. Possibly."

"I'm in."

"Me too."

"Spread the word to the others. The Angels will protect and defeat evil; we will endeavour to win at all costs!" Everyone cheered.

"And be fed with tea," and everyone cheered much louder than before.

Chapter Forty One

Inconveniently for Zed he saw the Thing too late. Rudely it didn't give Zed time to fight back and savagely engulfed him, suffocating Zed until he passed out. And that would have been that - if it wasn't a Thing. You see Things are not physical; they are not souls and not made the same as Angels or Demons. In people's dreams each night they exist, created in a complex form that is neither real nor imaginary. Drifting around nothingness, waiting for a human's sleeping brain to open a path to reality they infiltrate and fight to destroy their host's body before they vanish again in the morning. While most people sleep, unseen battles of epic proportions are raging between the sleepers' brains and Things. Fights last for hours. The warring parties battle to win reality. If the brain loses, it's game over for the human. Winning means the Thing can exist, it can escape. Remember the stories about bogeymen, monsters in your cupboards and other such horrors? These are based on the recollections of the few who have survived an encounter with a physical Thing.

During a battle, the Thing probes the brain looking for any part it can persuade the sleeper is real. To convince the human their dream is reality is how they win. But the brain is clever and hunts down the intruder. As soon as a Thing enters the brain it knows it's there. Each time the Thing accesses an open part of the neurological highway, SLAM, the brain shuts the door. This can go on all night. Restlessly the sleeper will be tossing and turning, never relaxing and in the morning will feel exhausted. All this is worth it though as the brain will emerge the victor. But as the brain gets older and weaker, sometimes the brain loses. The sleeper will never wake and the Thing becomes real.

Real Things that have a physical form, like the one that attacked Zed, need physical contact with their victim so they can access a brain. But a brain can still fight a real Thing.

Knocked down on the floor, the Thing was wrapped around Zed and if anyone had been passing and witnessed the encounter, they would have seen a black splodge blurred and constantly moving. Imagine a cloud pumped full of oil and spinning around like a dog chasing its tail.

Zed's brain was not happy. To state it more accurately, his brain was peed off. Relaxing, on autopilot for the last few hours, it had planned to rest for a few more. Not for years had Zed's angry brain engaged in combat to fight a Thing. A child's brain is a juicier target and, once an adult, many a human will never experience another attack. Years without practice hadn't made Zed's brain forget how to fight though; doors were being slammed shut as the Thing probed. Every time the Thing thought it was in, another door closed.

Remembering the euphoria of winning a battle, Zed's brain stepped up its defence. For Zed's brain was a master at defeating Things. Not because it was a particularly clever or cunning brain; no, it's because Zed and his brain loved sleep. Anything that upset a good night's sleep was a sworn enemy. Hence the brain had paid special attention to Thing defence tactics and, over the years, become a certified expert.

Such was his brain's confidence, it started playing with the enemy. No longer just defending itself but teasing the Thing. Anticipating the next attack, it left doors open, looking defenceless, enticing it and then slamming the door shut at the last second. All around other doors were slammed until the Thing had no exits. It was trapped. Knowing it had won, a huge burst of joy was spread through Zed's body stirring him once more.

And just like that, Zed woke again. Physically he had no scars, but he felt drained.

"Oh how annoying, I must have just fainted." Strangely, Zed thought to himself, he felt happy, which confused him greatly. "It's all this walking, I must find some transport that's not related to donkeys or my feet."

As so often happens, coincidentally, a camel walked past. "And not a bloody camel, thank you very much."

The women accompanying the insulted camel felt confused. "Sorry sir, you do not like camels?"

"I'm so sorry, just thinking out loud. Could you help? Is there any way of getting to the snail hole without walking? See, my feet are rebelling and refusing to take me there."

"I knew it," one of the ladies said, "you're a lazy foreigner, always moaning about walking."

Zed considered rebuffing this claim but, after digesting the information, he had to agree it was factually sound.

"You could try the logs, dearie", said another

"The logs? I think you misunderstand. Is there say a horse with a very soft saddle or a coach to get me there?"

"You misunderstand us, me laddy. The logs down at the taxi station."

"Ah taxi, that sounded more like it. No more walking for me. Where may I find this taxi station?"

"You'll have to walk there," they sniggered.

"Yes suppose I will," Zed said, dropping his head. "But it's for the greater good."

They gave him detailed yet confusing directions and eventually he found the place. A great sign declared his destination was called "Log-tax-tic" which took Zed a good minute or two to decode the awful pun.

There was an obvious queue, like most taxi ranks, and Zed joined the back waiting to see what sort of log taxi would turn up this time.

Not having to wait long to find out, rumbling sounds, like a bolder rolling along a dusty path, slowly grew louder. "It's amazing," he said out loud.

The guy in front turned round. "What's amazing?"

"Oh, just how logs are used for everything."

Zed was confronted by a face filled with shock and incredulity. "Well, yeah. How else would you move things?"

"Sorry, not from these parts. We tend to not roll logs much."

"Ah a traveller. I'm Maraavi. Good to meet you."

"Oh, nice to meet you too," said Zed, shaking hands. "I'm Zed."

"Sorry, did you say Zed?"

"Yes, strange name but my parents must have liked it."

"Not Zed, who stood up to Peter and opened the gate to heaven himself?"

"I, er, no I don't think so. He let me in after we had a chat."

Bouncing from foot to foot, Maraavi's excitement could be heard in his voice. "You are you. I can feel it. Oh Zed, I did not believe. Please forgive me."

He fell to his knees and begged out loud. Well begged after yelping from banging his exposed knees on the floor.

"Get up, get up. You're making a scene."

Looking up from his knees he said hopefully. "Do you command me to get up?"

"Yes. Now! It's embarrassing. Has that silly Bob been telling porkies round here?"

"Brother Nigel came and gave several sermons about your predicted arrival here and your need for help. He learned it from a brother Bob whom you speak of."

"Oh lord!" Zed thought looking round at the queue and passing people hoping that no one else had fallen victim to Bob's lies. "How has he managed to do this?"

"Well, you can forget about all that. What he says is rubbish. I am just Zed and want to catch a taxi." Zed had been through some strange situations in his life but this topped it. Totally confused and a bit panicky that Bob was spreading strange stories around heaven, he just wanted a taxi and normality.

"You command me to get you a taxi?" The guy's face looked like a dog begging for a treat from its master.

"I can't command anyone. I'm just Zed. Bob is just confused."

"You shall command me. Please command me."

"Oh, if I must, but just get me a taxi by letting me wait my turn in this queue"

"So, I just sort of do nothing?"

"Yes, that would be splendid."

"That doesn't seem right. No, it's not. You are the foretold one." Without warning he grabbed Zed's hand and moved with purpose along the queue. "Make way. Your saviour and leader is here, kneel down and let him pass."

The queue parted more out of shock than obedience. Normally people move out of the way if the person asking has the tendencies of a maniac.

At the front, an old woman was collecting her bags ready to mount her taxi. She was frail and slow. Bent over, she carefully sorted her bags and started to lift. When she'd finally straightened her body she was shocked to find her taxi gone. Convinced it must still be there, she stretched out her hands and prodded around. In the distance, if she had looked, she would have seen the dust and sand thrown in the air from Zed's speeding log taxi. Leaning out the side Zed frantically shouted out apologies that the woman could not hear.

Something else that could also not hear, was the Thing. For what happens to a Thing trapped when the host awakes? It disappears into nothingness. What did not exist, exists even less.

Chapter Forty Two

The clouds darkened, the wind swirled and everyone who saw it felt confused. Never before had anyone witnessed rain in heaven and when something happens that has never happened before, rumours start riding with the wind. The rumours grow and as they grow rumours come alive. They pass from person to person. The weak rumours die but others carry on growing - and their whispers can travel for a lifetime. The one that rode in the driving seat of the winds talked of evil and the Devil's work. Rumours can breed fear and panic - and heaven was not used to this.

Chapter Forty Three

There is a rule of thumb, adhered to by most, that all good plans with multiple action points, require a dedicated co-ordinator. Someone who keeps tabs on progress, knows what's happening and monitors completion. Plans can get out of control, spiralling into chaos without such coordination. Unfortunately for the Devil he was no such master coordinator. Once one part of a plan was made his thoughts would stray to the next part, bored with his first idea and never giving it a second thought. And so it was with his latest and most cunning plan – code named 'The Apple has landed' - which now, as it was unfolding, held no thought in the Devil's mind.

No one in charge had informed the 'implementers' that Zed was not going home. But it had dawned on the little dweeb exec, who came up with such a cunning plan, that perhaps it was best to let the waiting demons know that no such plan would be taking place after all, and they should return to hell. "Always best to help out the Devil and keep in his good books", he prudently thought.

Arriving at Zed's house, he was unable to locate the demons so decided to take a look around before resuming his search. Opening the front door, as in heaven front doors do not require locks, he thought to himself what an awful home to build when you could have anything you desired. The house itself was still empty, naked of furniture or fittings. Not bothering to look round he headed straight into the back garden. Where once there was just lawn and a wooden shed masquerading as a bar, there was now a pond. Shaped roughly in a figure of eight with a stone bridge spanning over the middle. The Dweeb, enjoying the fresh air of heaven, walked across the bridge and stopped in the middle to throw a few stones he'd subconsciously picked up. The water rippled its mesmerising circles from where the stones had landed; goldfish swam to the surface thinking food was on offer. From his vantage point, he now noticed the apple tree planted directly in the centre of the garden. Low, long, sturdy branches almost shouted out to be climbed.

Hidden, camouflaged high in the apple tree, patiently waiting, was a brown snake of no distinct features. Now, if you happened to say to the snake what a fine day it was and the snake replied: "Why sir, the day is a grand day indeed," then you could discern its vocal features were distinct from other snakes. Mainly down to the 'being able to speak' feature. But its appearance was more your smart, casual than black tie. The snake sat silently, watching the small, creepy looking man throwing stones at the defenceless pond. "At last," it thought, "he's here."

The dweeb, in days gone past, some hundred years ago, was quite a tree climber. Now he was finding out he was not so anymore. The first attempt resulted in a jump, a scramble and a bruised behind. His second was more successful; pulling himself up onto the lowest branch, he now sat swinging his legs and generally enjoying life in heaven. Having a snake sneak up from behind and hiss in his ear, was not what he expected. Even though he had planned the snake, it still took him by surprise. 'Expect the unexpected' they say, or in this case it is more apt to say 'unexpect the expected'.

"Aghhhhh!"

The world, for the dweeb, now presented itself the wrong way up. Gripping on for his life, he was precariously hanging upside down on the branch.

"Hello Zed. I've been expecting you."

"Helppp! Get me down someone."

"Do not worry Zed. You are safe with me. I am your friend."

Using a last ounce of strength, the dweeb hauled himself back up onto the branch and hugged the tree trunk for safety.

"You rude snake. You sneaked up and almost made me fall. I could have died. Well, apart from it's impossible to die here that is"

"I am sorry Zed but I needed to tell you something. The most important words you will ever hear"

"Zed? Oh you stupid snake. I'm not Zed. I'm here to tell you Zed is not on his way, so get back to hell."

The dweeb looked at the snake with contempt.

"I was told you would deny who you are. But I know Zed, you are yourself. See that juicy red apple within easy reach?"

The snake had wanted to make an epic speech about the apple but with such a long boring wait he'd forgotten most of it.

"Yes, you idiot. That is the red apple – the one I instructed to be out there to tempt Zed. And I am not Zed so go away."

The snake was impressed. This Zed bloke seemed to possess a talent for mind reading.

"Then Zed you will know that one bite of that tempting red, shiny apple and all you dreams will be true. Your eternal desires will be fulfilled. Your…."

"Yes, and I will turn to stone. So no, thank you. And one last time, I am not Zed," pointing his finger threateningly towards the snake's eyes, "and if you don't shut up I will report you to the boss."

Panicked, not at the thought of being reported to the boss but that Zed somehow knew about the dangers of the red apple, the snake made a decision. He knew that the instructions were to trick and tempt Zed but this was always his contingency in the back of his mind. Faster than you'd expect a snake to move he slithered up to the red apple pulled it from the tree with his mouth, making sure he did not bite it, and at break neck speed flung himself, like a flying tree squirrel, at the dweeb's open mouth. The apple, perfectly aimed, was forced into his mouth and the natural reaction was to bite down as it entered. Out poured the juice of the apple, seeping into the dweeb's mouth.

An observant bystander may have heard a very muffled: "Oh bollocks" just before the dweeb, starting from the mouth, turned a lovely shade of grey and into stone. Spreading until his whole body was a grey stone statue.

The snake, pleased with himself, called out to the waiting demons: "Come on lads, melt his soul down and take it to hell."

Chapter Forty Four

Highly embarrassed and pretty fed up, Zed sat holding on for dear life to his log taxi. How in the world did it go so fast? People kept dashing from front to back, impersonating ping-pong balls. Next to him was this new, obsessed, super fan. Unsettling for Zed, Maraavi knew everything about his life so far in heaven, and what amazed Zed further, was that not one thing he said appeared correct. He'd tried protesting to the guy that he was a normal, boring man, with no claim to Jesus's throne. Nodding and knowingly saying how clever he was for denying this, and being incognito seemed the only response. So giving up, Zed sat in silence - observing and considering. He had manners, private school manners and pushing in front of old ladies is not what one should do. The taxi driver had said it would take two hours at least to get to the snail hole. 'Driver' being perhaps an incorrect description, as all he did was shout angrily at people. On second thought - saying he was the driver one hundred percent described this man, seeing as shouting angrily is what all paid drivers do back on earth. He didn't seem to be in direct control, but a 'driver' he was.

As he sat watching Egyptian heaven go by, he started to relax. Having a comfy, cushioned seat behind his travel withered back, he sank slowly down melting into its comfort with pleasure. Feeling suitably relaxed, he began thinking. Thoughts dotted through his brain. "How the doodle did I get in here? Just a few days ago I hardly believed in heaven, yet next thing, large as life, chastising me was that rude Peter fella, claiming I was Hitler."

Unnerving for some, but for those who have studied scriptures, theorised or written great books on the subject of the glory and glamour of heaven's entrance, the actual reality has been known to make nuns faint and priests gasp. Battered old wooden garden gates - I mean really?!

Zed, lost in his own relaxed world, carried on in his wandering thoughts. I've built my dream home, met an Angel and even been cursed. Amazing.

To achieve things, when still young, will bring praise and in some cases greatness. Achieving death early, is not so celebrated. The part of the brain that had kept quiet so far, decided it was time to intervene a little. But I died early. I miss my friends, I miss my dog and I miss my bed. Uncontrollably, he burst into tears. The emotion was buried deep, but slowly it increased in pressure, day after day, until now. Like a champagne cork had been released from its bottle, it shot out memories, spraying them forth, soaking Zed with his past life.

Hysterically emotional, Zed required a jolt to pull himself together. A 'keep your chin up, sonny' encouragement but multiplied to the moon and back. There are many ways people snap out of their emotional breakdown. What happened to Zed can concretely be confirmed as a one-off technique. Through his blurry, tear covered eyes, Zed suddenly noticed that the person next to him - and he had to double-check this before believing the facts - was calmly collecting his tears in a bottle.

"What, good man, do you think you are doing?"

"Sorry, sorry. I prayed to the Lord to give me strength to resist my urge and I failed. I have relented to greed and collected your tears, the tears of the saviour. They say they can bring good luck when bathed in."

"Stop being ridiculous. Why do you think I am your saviour?" Zed said almost threateningly.

Beaming from both corners of his mouth he told Zed. He repeated the sermons that made women faint and children cry, the horrors that were foretold. The pain and suffering and how a great man would enter heaven to save all. How he would put Peter in his place and make a dangerous trip to fight the Devil to the end.

Half amused and half annoyed, Zed listened flabbergasted until the end when he half choked, half screamed.

"The Devil? Is he real? I mean, I know now heaven is, but is he real?" Resonating terror, his voice stuttered uncontrollably.

Images of horror, straight from childhood are infinitely easier to conjure up in one's brain than joyous scenarios. People laying in the dark do not look at shadows and wonder at the shapes formed, whether a friendly fairy or cuddly animal is waiting to spring out and cheer the night up. No! they think instinctively that it's a monster, a horrifically evil monster, intent on killing and being an all round bad sort of horror. This was the same with Zed and hell. He knew what terrors may lurk there - vile, disgusting creatures, ready to inflict pain and suffering for eternity. Whereas, heaven drew no instant images of joy. A good deal of concentration would have been needed if someone asked Zed to describe heaven prior to his arrival in God's kingdom.

Maraavi confirmed the worst. "He is. People have told me the Devil will attack heaven one day."

"But how would I fight him?"

"Use your powers. The scriptures say you will overcome Satan with untold powers. I understand you are reluctant to let a insignificant soul like myself know your secret powers." Pushing his luck, Maraavi sheepishly asked: "If you did want to though, I'm all ears."

"No I don't want to tell you. Hold on, what am I on about? I have no powers!"

"Ok, I only asked." Half annoyed that Zed refused, Maaravi looked teenager like - in a strop.

"Look. It's a nice story told by a mad idiot but I'm afraid it is a fabrication, based on a misunderstanding I had with Peter at the gate. I have no powers and I'm not your saviour. As far as I can see, no one needs saving apart from me with my curse."

"You're cursed?"

"Yes, by a mummy."

Maraavi screamed in terror and dived off the log taxi without warning. Zed heard something about curses being infectious as Maraavi rolled on the floor.

"That must have hurt." Chuckling to himself, Zed looked back at the man running away, arms flailing. Concluding correctly that, as he was in ancient Egypt, most are bound to be terrified of curses.

Now back to his thoughts, Zed was annoyed that people knew who he was. Hopefully the story would not spread. For someone who enjoyed being on the outskirts of attention, people knowing him and thinking he was the saviour brought cold sweats to his body. And as for the Devil being real! That was scary. Imagine fighting the Devil. He wondered how long he would be able to run before being squashed like an ant on the bottom of a giraffe's stiletto.

Requiring a distraction, Zed wondered if the internationally recognised language of the taxi driver stretched to heaven.

"Been busy tonight, mate?" Not a sentence a private education encouraged, but when in a taxi, speak their native tongue was Zed's view.

"Slow earlier but picking up now." Swiftly followed by "Stopppp!!".

Like an uncaught pancake, Zed splattered onto the floor of the taxi, cowering, worried he'd offended the taxi man.

"What's happened, have we crashed? Is it the Devil?"

"What you on about the Devil for? We are at the snail hole mate."

Jumping down, Zed thanked the driver and his crew and set off. They were in open desert country once more - bleak, featureless surroundings with no notable characteristics. To give describing the featureless a go: there were spherical grains of minute properties, each a browny orange shade, all packed together as if they were penguins attempting to keep warm. Millions upon millions of penguins slowly moving around, tossed in a gentle breeze, some flying up, trying to reach the blue sky, before falling back amongst the millions.

There was one feature not so featureless though. Unless you looked in the right direction and from the correct angle, then you might miss it. It was shimmering, like a mirage in the distance - a whopping great tunnel. Being a taxi driver of great integrity, the decent chap dropped Zed off in a position where the tunnel could be easily seen. Many a rogue taxi driver had left their fare payer roughly near the tunnel, leaving the person to never find the entrance.

Noticing another failure in heaven's administration, Zed made a mental note to suggest appropriate footwear be provided on entrance to any of heaven's deserts. His heavy, sweaty trainers seemed to fill up with sand - inexplicably before they made contact with any.

Once again, seemingly for the umpteenth time, he set off to cross a desert. Slow progress gradually reduced to a crawl, with every few yards involving a sand-shake ritual from his shoes. While on one of these 'pit' stops, Zed's eyes zoomed in on the tunnel. This took far too much brainpower for Zed's liking. If he moved his focus a nanodrop either side of the tunnel it faded away and only a slight haze could be seen. The sort of haze you get on a hot day but only where the tunnel once was. Thinking about it, Zed remarked to himself that it seemed mighty good luck actually noticing the thing in the first place. With staring abandoned, he carried on.

Getting ever closer and focusing on the tunnel again, Zed saw he had missed something. About a metre in front there was a sign with an arrow pointing towards the mouth of the snail hole. Printed on the sign were some helpful directions - helpful for the extremely short-sighted anyway. 'Snail Hole - One Metre'. On the other side of the tunnel sat a park bench. Drawing closer, he could see embossed on a brass plaque attached to the bench, 'In loving memory of Frank'. A nice touch you may think, someone had lovingly erected a bench for their beloved. However, when thought about, this bench raised many questions. Firstly and most importantly, how did someone die in heaven? On entering the tunnel this played heavily on Zed's worry genes.

Snail holes are a mysterious anomaly - either a genius design or a natural phenomenon, no one knows. Observers see what appears to be a tunnel. It certainly has an entrance and you could see and walk through it, but walking around the back where there should be a solid barrier, which would enclose the tunnel, there was nothing. In fact the whole thing just disappeared. Although, walking in, you'd find a three-dimensional space, from the outside the tunnel had, very much, a two dimensional structure. Only when looking directly, from the front of the entrance, could you see it. The entrance was constructed from large, grey rocks, creating an eye-pleasing arch, spanning a good ten or twenty metres but wide enough to fit several elephants side by side - although whether that was a consideration in the design is not known.

So this was it then - the snail hole. Zed attempted for a few seconds to answer the question that could never be answered - 'did God mean this to be here and how did the dimension's paradox work' - before declaring it's here so what's the point in wondering? Zed's brain had enough going on already and had been deprived of alcohol for far too long, so it gave up and signalled for the legs to forward march.

Flooring was catered for with (surprisingly some may say) block paving. Zed walked through the very badly laid, half finished, block paving floor. What appeared nicely constructed from afar, close up looked amateurish and dangerously wobbly. This led on after twenty metres or so to the next bit of the path, an industrial looking, black, tarmaced surface with great chunks crumbling away. One would suggest the pathway had been laid by unskilled builders.

Unquestionably impossible, the tunnel neglected to obey the rules of construction and did not possess a roof. On looking up, the sky could be seen; all blue with some grey clouds skimming along by the wind. If Zed was well versed in the language of wind then he would have heard angry voices and mutterings of moths. Perhaps because of its rebellious behaviour with the lack of roof, the tunnel did have two firm walls to give an air of normality. A silvery-grey, slimy stone high as the sky stood firm on either side. What was on the other side, if anything, no radiography or drilling program would ever discover.

Momentarily, in awe of the place, Zed carried on down the hazardous driveway. The tunnel emitted spooky vibes and Zed's nerves were rattled with the talk of the Devil and the plaque on the bench. A loud bang, from somewhere in the distance, hit his nervous system, a strike more powerful than a supernova. He dived for cover but noticing there was nothing to take cover under, he chose the starfish-flat-face-to-ground technique. On the ground he could hear some distant rumbling and, using the well-documented technique all film stars use, he placed his ear to the ground. Strangely, he thought he could hear what sounded like a construction site. Certainly something pneumatic and the classic call sign of a builder, wolf whistling, was just about audible. Rising to his knees he squinted hard into the distance and, sure enough, Zed could swear he saw men in high vis jackets. Feeling more relaxed with fellow humans obviously constructing or fixing stuff, he got up and advanced at a canter. With the noise growing louder and even individual voices now being heard, it came as a shock, as he got nearer, that they seemed to disappear into thin air. Coming to a logical conclusion he identified the issue. It must be the lack of alcohol giving me visions.

Ahead, where once there were high vis vests, alcohol-deprived, induced visions, there now stood a mammoth of a great wall. That must be the exit he thought. But as he got closer he realised - there was no door.

Chapter Forty Five

"Things are looking up," thought the Devil happily as he calmly peeled a King Edward potato at blistering speed ready to roast. Becoming addicted to TV shopping channels, Satan owned quite an extensive array of impressive cooking gadgets. Most of them useless, but his easy peeler was truly amazing.

Word had arrived an hour before, via carrier pigeon, of the demons' success at Zed's parents' home. Carrier pigeon being the greatest form of communication ever invented. The stupidity of imagining that a bird would ever deliver a message, is only matched by the impossibility that it actually works - combining to make an unbeatable winning score in any game of 'communication top trumps'.

Taking a second potato - this time a Jersey - he spoke to himself. "The four incompetent demons will have been noticed by the bigwigs up above, that's for sure. They will all be off snitching about hell interfering in heaven again. Good."

In front of him, on a table, lay the new plans he'd been sent earlier outlining the technical schematics for the great snail hole wall. They showed an impenetrable fortress, built to withstand earthquakes, bombs and anything else that could be thrown at it. Checking them one last time the Devil smiled knowingly.

Chapter Forty Six

Resorting to the age-old trick known throughout all realities of sitting down and leaning against a wall, Zed had heroically given up. He presumed it would take years of unrelenting pain to walk all the way to his parents without the snail hole. Zed huffed in frustration - just his luck; for some unknown reason a wall to be built blocking the way. Perhaps this was evidence to show God did not intend these short cuts through His heaven and had commanded there to be a wall built to block said snail hole.

Most builders, architects and surveyors would agree that to construct, from scratch, a wall ten feet deep and a mile high could not possibly be built in a few hours. How could a wall be constructed at such speed, magic perhaps? No, what about slave labour? Wrong again. What you require is access to thousands upon thousands of cowboy builders. Now your classic, run of the mill, cowboy builder collects the money and gets the job done as quickly as possible; if the job is going too slowly, they take the executive decision to move onto the next project leaving the last to build itself. Their incentive to build so quickly - or on more occasions than not, to leave the project part built - is money - money that will not be taxed. Hell, like heaven, has no currency so this wall commission brought no incentives to these cowboys. For them, the aim was clear: complete the job as quickly as possible expelling minimum energy. Only the fear of the Devil's punishment motivated them to build at all. So they had built the wall not wanting to feel the wrath of Satan's anger, and it looked pretty impressive from where Zed was looking.

An imposing, impenetrable, awe-inspiring image of a wall met Zed's eyes. Now step through, metaphorically, this wall and a rather less positive scene can be beheld. Anyone viewing from the other side would notice some underlying faults. To start with the wall's foundation was indeed technically ten feet thick, like the design; it was just that only the first layer of bricks was ten feet thick. The remaining construction consisted of a single layer. Again, from the front, the pointing had been completed but, from the back, you could see the missing cement. Cowboy builders are amazing. Amazingly crap.

Zed's brain was in a twist. What to do? Knowing cursed humans tend to end up in bad luck situations gave Zed a carrot to chase. However, the stick beat him hard with the thought of walking. Trying to contemplate walking the long way round hurt his head - and actually physically accomplishing this would induce a feet rebellion. In fact, the feet were screaming in protest already. The brain being the cleverest part of the body was getting annoyed. As far as it was concerned, the other parts did what it said. There was no democracy; just a dictatorship and quite aptly the rest of the body thought the brain was a power crazy prat and wished it would sail off in a ship. But the brain definitely had more brains, so it took action sending a signal, or command, down to left foot - that Zed was extremely angry and to kick the wall to release his anger. The foot obliged. The foot screamed in pain. The brain laughed. Next time shut up when I'm trying to think.

Pain filled his left foot. To combat this Zed hopped about cursing every moon under and over the sun.

There are those who claim that when in pain hurting another part of the body can take the pain away. In a few seconds Zed would know that's a load of nonsense.

"Oww!" A brick had fallen from the sky landing as if aimed, like a peach of a shot, onto Zed's right foot. This did little to relieve the pain from his left. A passing observer would comment on Zed's acrobatic abilities, hopping from one foot to the next in a mad, panicked, pain-inflicted dance.

Zed's brain was loving it. It only meant to get revenge on one foot and now both were suffering. It was enjoying this so much, for a laugh, it decided to get some well-deserved revenge on the hands for offences dating back many years. 'Punch the wall,' was the message it sent.

Zed punched the wall.

"Oww. Why did I do that?"

He was now hopping while shaking one hand furiously.

Woosh bang.

Another brick fell and this time the debris flew past his head.

The brain retreated deep into its home within the skull. A bit too close that one. Best not push my luck, and signalled to sit down on the floor and recover.

Energy zapped from his crazy dance, Zed sat down in pain. Although his feet were throbbing and fist stinging, there seemed no logical reason to Zed for having problems with his vision. Staring at the wall suggested either **he** was swaying or the wall was. Perhaps he had taken a direct hit on his head causing some blurriness in his vision. Or the wall was wobbling. Confused, he turned around and looked the opposite way but nothing was swaying. He looked back and forth several times until his brain had stopped laughing at the previous events and started listening to the panic part of the brain that screamed urgently: "Run!" And run he did.

The wall was indeed swaying. It was resonating to its own rhythm, slowly speeding up the tempo. The thing with really tall, really skinny objects is, once they start wobbling, it's hard to stop them. Like the Irish, Zed had some luck; the wind was blowing away from him. The tunnel acted as a funnel for the wind to flow, seemingly sucking air through with quite a force.

Still in full running mode, Zed heard an almighty crash. Like the sound of a ten mile high wall falling - that sort of sound. A noise so great and loud that theoretical scientists have since suggested it could be heard on earth. Others say that's just stupid.

Although only one brick thick, ten miles of brick falling at once still creates a tremendous amount of energy, and that energy needed somewhere to escape to. The ground sent a tsunami of vibrations taking all the colossal energy with it. Outpacing Zed - similar to a cheetah racing a stone - the wave caught Zed in a microsecond, flipping him off his feet and into the air.

"Oww!" screamed his brain after landing square on his head. Never a believer in Karma, the brain had to admit this was compellingly good evidence in its favour.

Chapter Forty Seven

History is littered with professions despised by others. From executioners to politicians, these are the people that get left in a corner at dinner parties or much later in life - or more precisely in lifeless times - get left in hell. Nowadays the once noble job - but now overrun with mindless muppets - of project manager has taken on the mantel of 'most loathed job'. Anyone having the misfortune of dealing with a project manager knows it's hard to feel sympathy. But as Rich Wyatt walked nervously towards the Devil's office, it would take a man with no heart not to feel a tinge of sadness. Dressed in a smart, shiny, grey suit, matching purple shirt and tie, with brown, 'look-at-my-face reflection' polished shoes he perfected the image of a trainee, wannabe project manager.

"Enter!" the Devil roared even before Rich had knocked. Gripping the doorknob, his hand shook as though holding a pneumatic drill; he just about managed to gain enough grip on the rough, old wooden doorknob to open the huge, heavy door.

"Excellent, on time and with good news to report I'm sure."

Rich looked remarkably similar to a person desperately trying to hold in a wee. He felt more like someone desperate not to be used as the Devil's personal toilet.

"How did the wall build go? I expected good things from you."

Rich found a second, in these worrying times, to wonder why he expected good things. Through this brief career, he had managed to cock up every project he was involved in. He could not be faulted on effort, yet the results? Well, the best thing to say was that there were results - just not the ones any of his project's had projected. All the results were there, just not in the right order.

"The build went to schedule and was completed on time." This was true. No one could argue the tight deadlines to complete on time had been hit, yet he knew this was just delaying the inevitable point in time that the truth would come out.

"Excellent. You inspected the wall after completion?"

"Yes."

"And was it to plan?"

"Technically yes, and they added a few driveways."

"Well, they will come in useful for all the cars in heaven won't they?"

Could he detect some irony in the Devil's voice?

"Have we had a report back confirming the wall stopped Zed and he is now this very moment on his way home, having given up any hope of reaching his parents?"

"To answer your first point, yes it stopped him."

"So he is on his way home?"

Here it comes; I'm going to have to come clean. "No. He pushed the wall over and is now on his way to his parents." Rich said this with the stance of someone tensing, ready for and knowing a punch is on its way. Eyes closed, face slightly turned and crumpled up.

"That is unfortunate. Tell me how did Zed, a mere mortal guy with no notable strength, destroy a wall like this?"

This took Rich by surprise. He was expecting a fate worse than a fate worse than death but the Devil seemed calm.

"He kicked it, Sir."

"That would explain it. Strong foot that Zed. Now run along to torture room six for an hour."

"Torture room six. That's not even that bad," thought Rich, running out the office before the Devil could change his mind.

Satan rose from his leather, spinning chair with added wheels (a feature that confused and angered the Devil) and went to his window. He was always conscious of keeping his office equipment current, so he still used the useless, moving seat. A seat is meant to stay still he had pleaded before giving in. He looked at his sea of fire, huge waves of flames crashing against the scorched black cliffs, mythical monsters rising to the surface, searching for a human meal. On the cliffs rows of humans, evil humans, the worst of the worst, waited for their turn to suffer. One after another they were all thrown into the sea, forced to swim through agonising pain until finally escaping to the other side. Screams of pain could be heard as they dragged themselves onto shore only to be pulled back up the cliffs and thrown back in. "Oh what a calming and awe inspiring sight," the Devil thought.

Turning his back from the fun of the window, he congratulated himself on hiring this Wyatt nob to manage the build. "Get an idiot to do a job and an idiot will always fuck it up. Just as I planned."

Chapter Forty Eight

Struggling to overcome the air's bumpy turbulence, the brown, fragile butterfly flapped its bright, exhausted, elegant wings one last time. Briefly halting, bringing calm to the air, the wind turned and laughed. Blowing with all the strength and energy stored, the wind flung the butterfly up and up, somersaulting the majestic creature high into the air before falling back down in an uncontrollable dive, crashing antenna first onto a soft, moss-covered pillow in the harsh rainforest floor.

"I don't need your tiny wings; you are but a squashable, insignificant moth. I am the wind. I can destroy trees, sink ships and feed fires." Before the annoyed butterfly could point out significant differences between itself and a moth, the wind had gone.

The butterfly looked up, bruised but not battered. "Oh how they forget where they came from so easily." It could have said, 'oh no, I've created a monster', but that it thought would be too obvious.

The wind raced on. It was almost strong enough now and knew, with an impending purpose, where to go.

Chapter Forty Nine

Unable to see past the dust particles floating around - reminiscing about when they used to be bricks - Zed sat on what he presumed to be the ground. It was certainly hard and flat - two key factors in identifying ground.

A good five minutes later the dust had at last started to clear and Zed felt sure, after near constant coughing, that most of the wall no longer lived in his throat. Fine tuned observation was not needed to notice two important points of interest. Firstly, the wall no longer stood where once it blocked the snail hole. Secondly, the whole tunnel was full of Egyptians, and each one skilfully carried more bricks than Egyptianaly possible.

Quite surprised, but too exhausted to be shocked, Zed asked: "Excuse me but where did you all come from?"

Looking miffed off that Zed had interrupted her from collecting rubble, the lady replied: "We heard the sound of building materials falling, and now everyone is desperate to claim the best bits."

"Of course", thought Zed, "they are obsessed with building. Amazing, they have now even evolved special hearing to find supplies of building materials. Darwin would be pleased that evolution is alive and kicking in God's heaven - and no doubt a little perplexed that God and heaven existed."

He sat there watching for an hour until the last brick had been collected. Noticing the error in the previous sentence, Zed picked up the actual 'last brick' that was almost completely hidden under sand. Tossing it into the air, his hands waited for the catch. But like a superhero – 'EgyptianMan' perhaps - a guy appeared from nowhere, caught the brick at the peak of its parabolic curve and sped off. And again he was by himself. "They do love building."

He did mean to ask someone if they knew why the wall was there but everyone was too preoccupied to stop for a chat.

"Well, best get on then. No point sitting around." Most people would perhaps be in shock, a near death experience, swarming brick hoarders and 'EgyptianMan', but Zed, as in life, brushed off anything unusual and carried on - plus the hard ground was not being enjoyed by his behind.

As heaven is flat, there is no horizon so the eye can see for miles. Far in the distance he could make out what appeared to be the end of the tunnel, but with no way of estimating the distance, he knew not how long it would take to reach. Having no water, no food and no alcohol put a damper on things and an extra demoraliser to the recipe of doom, he was travelling to see his parents who despised him. Oh, and he had a curse as well. Zed set off in a sulk.

Progress initially speeded up, with Zed no longer hopping over missing bricks or tripping over crumbling tarmaced driveways. The surface this side of the fallen wall defaulted to sand. Never in his life did Zed think he'd hate sand to the point of declaring each and every grain a sworn enemy. Too many hours of rough sand under his feet had changed it from bringing back memories of times spent as a boy on beaches to now pure hatred. "Not much further," he thought as the large exit came closer. Judging the distance became easier and he estimated another ten minutes until re-entry into official heaven once more.

About this time, Zed noticed the angle his body currently occupied. Head down, back bent forward; in most situations this would have resulted in a blooded nose from the impending face plant into the floor. Only the strong, unnoticed force of the wind kept him standing. Now his senses awoke and his brain kicked into action. Alarm bells were ringing in his ears that this was abnormal. The wind had really picked up; Zed's estimated exit time needed some serious re-calculating. Slowly he was fighting his way through the pounding wind. Orphaned gusts of rebellious winds that had escaped from the main body, started to pelt Zed as he walked. Sand hitched lifts with the wind and like swarming bees it circled him, teasing its captive victim, waiting for the moment to attack, and then with ferocious speed disembarking from the wind, millions of sand particles flung straight into his face.

Zed had been walking for a few hours and hadn't really noticed. Still deep in his sulk and with his unique skill of managing to ignore most things, it was only now that his facial pain receptors screamed in agony, kicking the brain into action. "Oh bother!" was the strongest words Zed could think off. But he was in a lot of bother! Within five minutes the wind created a storm of sand. He couldn't see further than his hands and he really had to bend forward to push through the wind. His mouth, eyes, ears and nose were now home to sand, dirt and brick dust blocking all routes for oxygen to enter. Gasping for air, he struggled on. A great flash of light lit up the path for a brief moment, followed by the rumble of thunder and the heavens opened. By this - just to clarify - heaven did not in fact open but rain poured down. To start with Zed was quite pleased. The sand was washed out of his head's orifices and helped him catch his breath. Filling his lungs with rapid deep breaths he thought that was it, the worst had been and he had not failed. But no one turned off the tap. The breaths that filled his lungs now contained less air and more water. The ground beneath him grew soggier and harder to walk in, with a custard-like texture sticking to his feet and sucking them down. The rain now took on the task to batter his face and nothing could stop the wind, still doing its best to blow Zed over. Wishing once again, with great regret, that he'd stayed at his bar, he wished he had not started his journey. But most of all, he wished he was not dead.

Each step required a Herculean effort to pull his foot out from the wet sand, force his leg through the wind and then drag the other leg to follow. He knew he couldn't die out here but he thought 'they' were having a jolly good go at 'killing' him, as he finally fell over flat on his face, unable to move anymore.

Chapter Fifty

Elemiah felt like she had been fighting a losing battle from the start. Maybe even before the start. Having been ridiculed, called mad and insulted in equal measures she wondered, 'what's the point?'. But she knew she was right. Zed may just be a nobody but this nobody was attracting a lot of attention from a somebody. Namely the Devil.

Recovering for a few hours, after being injured unfairly by Zed's oversized boot, she brooded in a favourite haunt of Angels. Strictly no humans were allowed. This was the sort of place Angels went to feel important. Most, although friendly with humans, looked down on them and almost felt jealous towards these 'things' that God loved so much. The Righteous Club, as this favourite haunt was called, could tell many a story if the walls could talk - which of course they could, to everyone's great annoyance. Always butting in to private conversations or more irritatingly, belting out a song in a discordant voice. Hearing the concept from one rock 'n' roll human fan, the idea had been formed to cover all the walls in egg boxes to soundproof those overly talkative walls. Following the instructions from a clever looking soul, thousands of egg boxes were nailed to the walls. This did nothing to dampen the sound of the wall or ability of the walls to talk and only achieved a messy puddle of cracked eggs oozing out of the boxes onto the floor. Angels, although clever, lack a lot in common sense.

While resting in the club, Elemiah spent her time hidden in a corner knowing other Angels would be talking about her mad-hat ideas. Every so often she'd hear her name mentioned and laughter dutifully followed.

Wanting to escape this verbal mockery and now feeling rested enough, she left and continued on to where she knew she had to go.

As she flew over Egypt she was surprised to see people running for cover, all looking for somewhere safe to shelter. The wind was causing havoc. Unlike the unfortunate humans, she could fly high above the effects of the rampant wind, avoiding its attention.

Knowing precisely where she was needed, Elemiah flew on with trepidation and vigour. An urge had been kicking away at her and now she was feeling it. Suddenly, changing direction, she dived down into the snail hole, briefly having to fly through the wind, which even for an Angel was hard work.

Once through she cursed. Angels hate getting their wings wet and now they felt soaked. She had entered the storm of the tunnel and quickly flew high enough to escape the rain. Halfway through the Angel stopped and hovered instinctively. Why had she stopped she thought, and then it hit her. She had seen Zed but it had not registered straight away.

Having fought bravely with the wind and enduring the rain, Zed had succumbed to the onslaught, battling for as long as he could, he now lay face first in the sodden sand, soaked, drenched and all round wet. Observers would have commented that the chances of escaping from the snail hole did not favour brave Zed. What was needed was a miracle.

Like a superhero from heaven, on went Elemiah's metaphorical superwoman pants. She dived, arms stretched out and grabbed Zed by his feet pulling him high in the air until they reached the calm atmosphere above. Zed, who had been drifting in and out of consciousness, was brought fully back to life, when he noticed the worrying fact of how high he was, upside down and flying. Looking up (or down, he wasn't certain which) he saw the Angel from the hotel. "Ah my guardian Angel," he said and fainted.

"If I'm right," she thought, "you'll need more than one guardian Angel to help you soon, and I'm not sure any more are coming".

Chapter Fifty One

Bob was on his way and was over excited. This was why God snatched his life away from him when still so young. He understood now. Destiny brought the meeting with Zed and fate would tell the story that had been foretold. Ever since realising he had a destiny to fulfil in the afterlife, people were listening to him; they saw him as their leader. For a leader he was and at this very moment he was leading about two hundred men and women towards the end. Every few miles they would absorb more into their ranks, 'zombified' or 'enlightened' (judge for yourself) by Bob's sermons. Bob preferred the word 'naturalised' to 'brainwashed' in the same way Vlad the Impaler preferred 'misunderstood' to 'psychopath'. People flocked to see Bob and were overwhelmed in his presence. He felt good. No, he felt better than good, he felt powerful.

Chapter Fifty Two

Cabin fever, that was what the Devil had caught. Except his cabin flowed with lava, stank of stale death and he was kept locked in there for eternity. Sometimes he thought his mind was slipping and perhaps gone a little mad. Once he'd spent a week wandering round hell counting every human just to pass the time. Eventually he stopped after realising the foolishness of the task, as new, damned souls entered at a quicker pace than he could ever count. The fact was, the Devil hadn't got out much over the last few years. Today he was visiting as much of hell as he could.

Housing hundreds of demons, a sea-of fire view with modern decor throughout, that's how the derelict block of flats he was gazing at was sold as an idea to the Devil. Now they were crumbling away, sinking deeper and deeper into the soft soil of hell. Someone overlooked the need for foundations and that someone was somewhere under the flat, punished for her mistake, to rot in the soil for eternity – an apt, devilish punishment, acting as a repair to the missing foundations. Next to the failed project a great cave stood. No ordinary cave but the first palace in hell. This cave became home to the Devil when he first entered his kingdom. Not through choice but necessity. Years of hard work, (well hard for the slaves), and detailed planning went into building what is now hell. The Devil for most part had forgotten how it used to be. Sitting on the warm rough floor, remembering the early days and how the simple things in death had kept him happy. A new soul to torture, or tending to his wasp nests - simple things like this had been enough. Now he wanted more. But there was no more in hell to be had.

Getting up and caressing the cave wall with his hand as he left, he wandered off towards the mouth of hell.

The general skyline of hell is an ever-changing view. With each new decade came new ideas and the Devil always wanted bigger and better. Cranes were an increasing eyesore, each rapidly building a new project, commissioned by the Devil. Where any new building was built, there would have been countless others knocked down before. Only a few original dwellings survived - all because of sentimental feelings the Devil had for them. There was the first statue built by thousands of Myanmar priests, all ferociously tortured every single second of every day to really increase work productivity, while carving the statue of Satan from stone harder than granite. Then there was the first church, built to worship the Devil - a crude construction made from slabs of rock - who commanded all must worship him there daily. He built it in a jealous rage when he heard about humans building such things for God on earth. His beloved swimming pool of blood was still there and regularly used by many a demon. They had tried building more impressive pools but none could hold the blood like the original. Another favourite and original feature was the garden of hell, the best and probably only nettle garden in any realm. Nettles grew ten feet high, lovingly tended by the Devil and a few green-fingered demons, all planted in neat beds which were weeded of any plants that might ruin the nettles' beauty. Wandering through, stopping at all these places the Devil knew he was right to do this.

Arriving at his destination, he remembered fondly how newly damned souls screamed in absolute terror if he were there to greet them personally. Now this was mostly done on a well-organised shift pattern, manned by some minor demons.

Pushing the current demon on shift out of the way, he waited.

The mouth of hell is a hole around five feet in diameter, of a colour that's not visible on earth; a colour that God had no design input into - an impossible pigment to describe. Only the damned who pop out through the hole will ever experience the colour. When a soul is sent to hell they very much go down, yet when they come out into hell they emerge going upwards - which makes no sense. If you were to put your ear into the hole - for a start your head would explode - but if you get past that potential inconvenience you would hear a sound comparable to the largest roller coaster being ridden through a swamp on fire - a blood-curdling, vomit inducing sound.

Hearing the imminent arrival of his next victim, the Devil posed in his most evil and frightening pose.

"Fear me you wretched, damned soul. Fear each day you will wake up in my great fire pit of hell. Screams won't be heard, forgiveness won't be answered; you have entered my kingdom and you will serve me for eternity. Unimaginable pain will be inflicted on you, your eyes will be ripped from your sockets, my demons will tear off your limbs, I will torture you and brand you with red hot pokers. Your nightmares will seem like dreams compared to what awaits you. You are mine and I will destroy you."

Roaring fire and thunder, he actually felt a bit guilty knowing the terror he'd just inflicted. Well, you can imagine his surprise to see a skinny, leather-clad, long-haired, piercing-hoarding, Devil worshipper springing towards him, diving and hugging his leg.

"My lord I am here. What do you command?"

"What the fuck?! Get off me!"

Swinging his leg, the guy was dispatched into the great sea while screaming in joy at the ride and shouting praise at the Devil.

"It's just not the same," he thought as he wandered back to his scheduled meeting. He knew he'd miss this place, but it was for the best.

Chapter Fifty Three

Running towards Jennings, his humongous, hairy, tail-wagging dog, Zed wraps his arms around the creature's neck and in return receives a slimy, wet, cold tongue to his neck.

Now they sit together in the local pub both consuming a Strogart bitter - one from a bowl and one from a glass.

Now watching the cricket, cheering as the opener goes for a duck. Then something strange happens - the ball has turned into a duck. Growing, expanding, changing colour and getting closer and closer to Zed. "I'm waiting for you," it says, millimetres from his face. Horns pop out and the duck becomes the Devil.

Zed was woken to the sound of a thud. Taking a while longer to ascertain the perpetuator of the thud like noise, the pain on his back soon informed him - the thud was from where he had been dropped and landed. Although 'landed' would imply a planned decent and this was not.

"Sorry about that Zed. Misjudged the height and dropped you too soon."

Rubbing his bashed head, he surveyed the view in front of him and smiled. A large billboard proclaimed he had made it. Clearly stated on the board were the words: 'Welcome to the Twentieth Century - Twinned with the Jurassic Zone'.

Never one to multi-task he now averted his attention to Elemiah. Her hair was a mess; she radiated the opposite of calmness and appeared very different to the first time they met. "I'm very thankful for you helping me and what a spot of luck you passing through the tunnel. What are you doing here anyway? Shouldn't you be at your hotel?"

Elemiah sensed Zed hadn't comprehended how much danger he was in. He just seemed to shrug it off as normal.

"I'm...," she said very slowly as she begged her brain to come up with an answer-of-genius, white lie. "I'm on a business trip. Looking to build a new hotel. You know, expanding the business. Never good to sit still in the hotel industry. And I must be off as I'm late for a meeting." Off she flew without a bye, or even worse a hug. Not looking back, she hoped he was convinced by her lie. Knowing Zed as she did, from the few times they'd met, she would say the chances were high he would be. He'd accept it and carry on.

"Nice lady Angel, that," Zed thought. "Saved my life and acted as if nothing happened."

Watching her majestically fly off, he noticed for a second time he no longer stood in the snail hole. She had dropped him off quite literally at the boundary of the zone that he wanted to be at. Looking back he could see desert stretching out for miles - but no sign or slimy trail of the snail hole.

Now that his life had been saved, dropped on his head from a great height and survived, Zed had two things to do. One, find his parents. But that could wait, so he actioned number two and headed off in search of a pub. Number two is higher than number one, so any rational person would prioritise a number two action over a number one. Nothing to do with alcohol - honest.

The road leading into the zone was pretty featureless. No awe-inspiring statues or breathtaking arches; just a basic paved path. In the distance a few skyscrapers dotted the horizon and, if one strained one's eyes really hard, a tall structure could be made out; a tall metal structure that one day, some hoped, would briefly house a rocket. Work began on the rocket as soon as the first few space pioneers started dropping like flies back on earth. Within a few years of death, they grew frustrated and bored, so set about the great space program of heaven. Beavering away, the construction rapidly progressed. With material and knowledge readily available nothing, it seemed, would stop the human race exploring heaven's final frontier. That is nothing, until a new engineer working in the program politely enquired what propulsion system they planned to use, considering that the combustion engine (and all other similar forms of propulsion) had been outlawed in heaven.

Further down the path, shops started appearing and soon he smelled the sweet smell that is alcohol and Zed entered the pub at third lane speed. Forgetting to slow, he hit the bar at some pace leaving his body slumped over it, arms stretched out in a desperate plea to be served. Taking pity, or believing Zed was a crazed madman, the barman pulled a pint without receiving the order and pushed it wearily towards Zed. Rudely, Zed grabbed the drink without a thank you and hurriedly poured the contents down his throat. The alcohol seeped out, finding its way into his bloodstream wasting no time at the liver. An excited brain could see the alcohol riding the blood, rushing towards its receptors and, like a shot of adrenalin, the alcohol seeped deep into the brain.

The effect on Zed was remarkable. He stood up tall, adjusted his clothes and no longer appeared mad. Thanking the nurse or barman or whatever he was, he ordered another in a more appropriate manner and took it back to a table. All the stress of the last few days lifted from his body. Even his donkey-bruised buttocks felt like new. It was amazing the effect alcohol had on Zed. Fully regrouped and recharged, and with the essential pub-finding task completed so successfully, he decided to divert some of his thinking power away from the choice of next drink and onto the location of his parents. "How the Devil do you find someone in heaven?"

Chapter Fifty Four

If it were possible to view all of heaven from above - which it is not for at least five reasons - the view would give any weatherman the weatherman equivalent of enlightenment. The whole of heaven was covered in dark, grey, threatening storm clouds, all circling like a gargantuan twister. You would have to zoom in several googleplexian of times to see the eye of the storm. There, there was only calm and sun. Anyone living in the eye would be oblivious to the havoc being raged across heaven - or what was on its unrelenting path towards its destiny.

Chapter Fifty Five

Zooming in and out of focus, the room adamantly refused to stay still. Life's simple questions now morphed into epic debates and the private school accent seemed to have cross-bred with a sloshing noise. Zed was drunk. Starting off with good intentions, Zed thoughtfully grappled to make a plan to locate his parents' home. It took a lot of brainpower to ponder a question such as this and, as anyone knows, brainpower is directly proportional to alcohol intake. Just a shame Zed again got the proportions the wrong way round.

With all the energy sapped from Zed's unathletic body - induced through heavy drinking and much thinking - the need for a nap grew. But where to lie down? Coincidentally, at this point, the answer fell from the sky - or at least appeared at the bar. While ordering his next drink a blurry image seized his attention. Seeing, or rather straining to focus on, a sign behind the bar boasting 'rooms with a view' he made the decision and stumbled over to the barman and enquired if any were available .

Zed and Jeff, the barman, had spent the last few hours chatting in between drink orders. From Jeff assuming at first Zed to be insane, they had grown to become good bar acquaintances sharing general pub chat and exaggerated stories. Jeff told the story of when God himself drank in the very chair Zed sat in. If pushed hard Jeff would have to admit his version of the 'facts' was stretching the truth into the realms of completely made up tosh. Namely the God part of the story. Anyway, as Zed got drunker, so he became more annoying. With Zed spluttering his words, spraying phlegm as he requested a room, Jeff felt the urge to lie and claim there was no room in the inn. But annoyingly, once in heaven people tend to do the right thing, knowing they owe at least that to their Maker as a thank you.

"Sure thing Zed. I'll give you the best room." Smiling, he shouted at someone and out came an employee. "Please show Zed to his room. Enjoy your journey. I mean night."

He was shown to his room by an old man who led him around a series of ups and downs and tricky-when-drunk corners. Zed could have sworn this swine of a man was taking a long, dangerous route, just to mess with him in his current 'one-too-many-drinks' condition. The corridors they went through smelt damp and lacked light. Stopping eventually the old devious man cackled something at Zed, no doubt an insult and opened the creaky door.

Once Zed was inside the room the old man left to find his next victim and Zed quickly found the bed. He performed a text book face plant onto the bed and entered the land of nod. Going to sleep is the same in heaven as on earth. You fall asleep then there is nothing. Sometimes there can be nothing all night until you wake but at other times the dreams, nightmares or Things find their way in. Zed this night was in the nothing zone for about ten minutes until his first dream entered. Humans tend to classify dreams as either dreams or nightmares, whereas Angel scientists have spent centuries experimenting on humans to formally identify the many types of dream that exist. Work stopped when using humans for testing became outlawed. Even before testing was banned, Angels were close to stopping it themselves. The pesky humans refused to keep still and never stopped their incessant moaning.

Each dream has characteristics that are unique. Like animals, all are different but some are similar. Many are nearly extinct but all are dreams. Zed's brain was entered by the life story dream, which unsurprisingly made the recipient dream about their life. This, as so often happens, was followed by a future dream. Like the great artist, L S Lowry's paintings – 'The Head of a Man' or 'The Park' to name just two - the naming conventions of dream studies were self explanatory.

Anyone observing Zed sleep, whilst dreaming his current dream, would see him smiling at his childhood, cringing as he went through puberty, grimacing as he struggled with adult life. Abruptly the dream ends and is replaced by another; the life story is almost always followed by a future dream. He dreamt about what might have happened; what could have been, if the grim reaper waking up late on that fateful morning had decided to miss Zed off his list, allowing him to catch up on his dutiful work. He dreamt of a wife, kids and growing old. It was a nice dream and his brain did not fight but encouraged the dream onwards; there was no danger this dream would attack like a Thing. Once the future had left, all was empty until just before morning. Another dream was trying to enter Zed's brain. The brain always checks the dream and either lets it in or pulls up the shutters, raises the drawbridge and barricades the doors. Knocking gently and patiently outside, an unseen, unknown dream floated. Bamboozled, Zed's brain felt confused. It had never seen a dream like this. What should it do? It took the safe option and started bolting all the entrances in case this was a Thing in disguise. But that brief moment of hesitation was all the dream needed; smashing through like a cannonball, darting in and then stealthily hiding. The brain knew it had got in but missed where it had gone. It waited for the dream's next move. Out it shot, darting along the motorway network of neurology, heading for the opening where it could play out the dream. Just making it in time, the dream paused to look over its shoulder. Big mistake. A true competitor never checks behind. Looking back is for losers. The brain was hot on the dream's trail and this brief pause produced the chance to catch up. Shouting something heroic, forgotten in the moment, it kicked the dream square on the backside and booted it back into the dream world.

Confidence shaken and ego deflated, the dream retreated. "Maybe next time," it thought, "I'll go for a pigeon. Always easy to infiltrate a pigeon." Although rudely evicted, without being given a reason, the dream had just about had enough time to play out in Zed's head. Not your normal movie type of film, more a slide show. Or as the Angels say, 'a flash dream'.

Zed woke up in a wet, sweaty panic. He had been nice and relaxed from his earlier dreams but this last one had panicked him - mainly down to the panicky nature the dream played out. It was simply an old man shouting loudly and quickly, over and over "library housing records" until the man was lifted into the air, flipping ungracefully round several times before flying out of sight.

Zed flung the covers off and shot out of bed, regretted the decision to arise so speedily and sat back down, head in hands with the familiar hangover feeling. Taking a second attempt at rising, he unsurprisingly waddled into another cold shower. Halfway through, when the cold painfully woke his brain up, he shouted out with much joy: "Bingo! I can check the library housing records for my parents." He stopped, confused and thought about it. How, he wondered did he know there were such records? And then he allowed his hangover to dictate the 'no more thinking rule' and went back to bed.

Chapter Fifty Six

Zed's mum and dad were fed up. It just wasn't on. They had been good, God loving people all their life and, rightly in their eyes, been rewarded with the greatest gift of all - heaven. But this was not in any bible they had read. Where did it say that once in heaven you could be kidnapped? Logic derives that kidnapping becomes an impossibility once in heaven. No bad, naughty, evil, depraved, sinister or malevolent people get to enter heaven. So kidnapping should be defunct. Quite an intelligent woman, Zed's mum deduced these gas men must originate from hell. "Maybe that's how they have a great sea of fire, as they have large gas reserves to burn," she pondered. "And if they are from hell, then the Devil needs to keep a closer eye on his people and make sure they're not running off to heaven for a spot of Sunday kidnapping". The whole situation really grated Cath's gears.

"I say, gas men. We are willing to have gas installed if you untie us. We won't even report your aggressive sales techniques to your seniors."

"We only have one senior and he enjoys being aggressive. Now shut up before I shut you up."

"Calm down Baphomet. You know the boss said not to harm them."

"I know," he snapped back. "But it's fucking hard with these disgusting goody two shoes here. Look at them still smiling even now. You won't be fucking smiling when your new Lord comes up to see you."

"On the contrary, I will smile like a rainbow if I ever get to see the good Lord."

Baphomet made a lunge for Zed's dad and was only just grabbed in time by Crocell.

"Stop winding them up dear," Zed's mum said. "I'm sure they will get bored soon of their silly game and leave us in peace."

Chapter Fifty Seven

Once a great fan and champion of the traditional naked look, the Devil now preferred a well-tailored suit. He had noticed his most evil residents in hell wore suits and, although he was not keen on them at first, he did like to keep up with trends. Standing next to a full-length, evil mirror he admired his newest tailored purchase. Poking out from the bottom of his perfectly fitted, luxurious, guanaco, double-breasted, grey, pin-striped suit were two extra pointy, Italian, black, shiny, soft leather shoes. These he was particularly pleased with.

Keeping up with trends admittedly was not the Devil's forte, and a few fashion crimes were broken along the way. He once even tried a bow tie. This seemed to have the unfortunate effect of people sniggering wherever he went and a Devil simply cannot be sniggered at.

Checking one last time that no creases ruined his suit's pristine look, he swaggered out feeling a million dollars. His plan for the day was: have a haircut and wet shave (which still bemused his barber as he had no hair - but one must do what the owner and bearer of evil tells you), and then a spot of lunch at his favourite restaurant followed by a stroll. Not just any stroll though. A stroll to his destiny - to the entrance.

Chapter Fifty Eight

Meat and two veg, or more precisely a greeny brown, sludge like substance with a suggestion of meat and two types of veg, presently sat on a cracked off-white plate, looking hideous in front of Zed. The sludge looked at Zed, and Zed looked back. Poking the less slimy part of the veg, he twirled it round with the fork hoping in a resigned effort that there could be solid broccoli within. Closing both eyes tightly shut and holding his nose, he begrudgingly ate all the so-called food knowing he required high energy levels for his day's work. Getting up, he thanked the landlord and gave the old fascist man, who directed Zed to his room the night before, a dirty look convinced that he had tried to make him fall or look like a plonker. The landlord helpfully told him how to find the library and gave surprisingly accurate directions. But knowing all directions are wrong, Zed ignored most and decided not to follow them correctly. This led yet again to getting lost several times.

More through luck than anything else, he stumbled upon the library and stood admiring it. The library seemed a grand old building, how a library was built before budget cuts. Nowadays, libraries are housed in buses and flimsy buildings. How the planners think they can hold all the knowledge and power that books posses in such easily escapable walls, is laughable. The knowledge and excitement seeps out, escaping the library. The books become less interesting and so fewer people visit. To attract more people to libraries, you first have to imprison the knowledge within. Staring up, Zed noted what a tall building this library was. Imposing pillars marked the entrance, and in Zed wandered. The inside opened up into a spacious open-plan reception area with dark oak wooden floors. Hanging on the walls were some large oil paintings of noble looking people, all covered in dust. Working on reception was an old man - a ridiculously old man. His name badge identified the oldie as Methuselah.

"Good day Methuselah."

The old man looked up. "Did you say something?"

"Yes, good day."

"What? Speak up boy."

"I said good day Methuselah."

"How you know my name?"

"It's on your name badge."

"What?"

Speaking very slow and loudly, Zed repeated himself.

"Oh yes I forget it's there. Did you want something? Or just here for an autograph?"

"Why would I want an autograph from you?" Zed thought. "No I'd like to locate the house of my parents," he said.

Ignoring Zed, Methuselah carried on: "It's just I'm quite famous."

"How can I locate someone's house?"

"I'm sure you've recognised me by now."

"Is there a way I can find out where they live here?"

"I'm in the Guinness book of records don't you know. Oldest man in the bible."

Zed gave up. "Could I have your autograph please?"

"Certainly not. You would have to come to my book signing which, coincidentally, is tonight," he said, handing Zed a leaflet.

Zed gave in. "My excitement and anticipation are beyond words and I will be gracing this event tonight but.."

"Get there early. There will be a big queue. Now, how can I help?"

"I am looking for my parents. A dream, I mean a lady told me I would be able to find their house address here."

"Looking for an address you say?"

"That's the one, yes, if you would be so kind."

"Then why didn't you say earlier? We could have found it by now. I don't know. The youth of today; always wasting time."

Zed thought about rebuffing this insult but wisely chose not to. "Could you show me how to find the address please, wise old man?"

"Yes, certainly. If you follow me we have the records of all homes built in our zone of heaven. Now you say a dream told you?"

Hastily Zed replied: "No, a woman. Definitely not a dream."

"Just want to make sure you are not mad before I show you round. No offence of course."

Zed went slightly red as he followed the librarian.

It has been noted by non-slugs that to walk slower than a slug is tricky. Methuselah however had perfected the technique and didn't even need to leave a slime trail. On several occasions Zed suggested he could go on alone, if given precise directions, but Methuselah insisted it was his job and no trouble at all.

"It's not far now," he said as they reached some stairs and started the climb to the summit.

Zed felt like a Sherpa helping a tourist up Everest. The old man was bound to have a heart attack - and how do you contact emergency help if he did? The next time he saw that Saint Peter, he would suggest all new heaven's residents be provided with a welcome to heaven booklet outlining important information such as this.

Seven breaks to catch his breath later, they had reached the summit and Zed mimed planting the British flag into the ground to celebrate.

"Here we are," said Methuselah. "When were your parents born into heaven?"

Zed had to think about this but worked out he meant when did they pass away. Giving him the date, Zed was pleased Methuselah appeared more focused on the task. He watched as the old man went through scroll after scroll, fingers working with ninja precision and at rocket speed.

Thirty seconds later and Methuselah held up a scroll in triumph.

"Then this will have the details."

"Smashing, old man. This won't take long going through. Is this scroll in alphabetical order?"

Methuselah face showed signs of confusion. "I think you misunderstood. This is just the one of many. I was looking for this one, as it's the first one. No reason to suggest your parents' details are within it though." He pointed to piles of huge scrolls. "Any of them could hold the details." With a great deal of skill he held the scroll he'd chosen with both hands and tossed it forward. The scroll unrolled along the floor in a perfectly straight line. It was depressingly long. "There is the name of every man, woman and child born in heaven that year with the address of the house they built."

Children of course, and babies too, unfortunately enter heaven as well as old people. God, who was not able to stop these tragic deaths, came up with a solution of sorts. They are frozen in time, as it were, and only unfreeze once their parents are in heaven. They are then reunited and get to grow up together. The gift of a family is given back by God. For God is eternally annoyed that he can do nothing to stop the young passing away on earth.

"But this will take me a year to go through," Zed protested.

"It's in date order so you can narrow it down and I can help until my book signing."

It took them over an hour but eventually they found it. Zed almost missed it, his mind scrambled after looking at so many names.

There, written in front of him, was his parents' address, and it hit him hard. He realised he hadn't seen them in over twenty years, that it had taken him ten to fully get over their tragic death and now he was scared to meet them. "Why would they not want to see me?" he thought, "we loved each other". A tear ran down his cheek that he quickly wiped before Methuselah could see.

Chapter Fifty Nine

Tired, and looking on the wrong side of bedraggled from battling that pesky wind, Elemiah circled Zed's parents' house high above, fretting.

Nothing seemed wrong, and that troubled her deeply. The house was there. Smack bang in the middle of where it should be. Where were the signs of danger, trouble or evil doings? No fires, screams or even loud noises. She started feeling a bit embarrassed. What happened if other Angels did bother turning up to protect heaven and all they saw was Zed meeting his parents? She would be ridiculed for eternity. Risking a closer look she flew down, keeping as quiet and disguised as possible. Still nothing. She edged, in a flying sort of edging way, closer, closer and stopped with nano seconds to spare just before a demon poked his disgusting face out of the door. She froze. He grunted, retracted his head back indoors and slammed the door.

Now the issue Angels have with suddenly stopping, is far less of a problem when on the ground than in the air. Elemiah may have frozen mid flight, but this didn't stop her shooting down towards the ground at high speed. At the last moment she remembered the importance of beating her wings and thus saved a demon-attention-grabbing thud on the ground.

Returning to the sky above, she felt like shouting: "Told you so, told you so" in joy that she was right, but she shuddered when she again realised she **was** right. What was that demon doing here? I need backup and quick. But will any Angels turn up?

Chapter Sixty

Zed thanked Methuselah and wished him good luck with the book signing. Knowing a fan when he saw one, Methuselah even gave him a signed copy, as Zed explained his family reunion would hamper his chances of attending later.

Exiting the library, Zed made a quick, mental checklist. He had the address, he had a map (quickly drawn on a scrap piece of paper) and he was off. But not for very long; outside was a pub. Now Zed has made this very mistake before and did not plan on making it again. What if this was the last chance of a drink before reaching his parents? No point in taking that treacherous risk. So he popped in and had a courage builder. Not staying more than ten minutes, he was off on his way again. "Nothing will stop me now," he thought as he strode on looking for the third tree on the right, knowing he had to turn at that point. He found it and found another pub. Zed's brain pleaded - what if the directions are wrong? We could be hiking for God knows how long. Best have another drink, just in case. In he went for a quick one. Back out again he went on. Nothing, and he repeated, nothing, would stop him now.

Five more pubs stopped him and instead of striding out from the last one, he stumbled out like a new born deer. Zed was drunk and only one minute away from his destiny.

"I am coming mother," he said out loud, slurring most of his words and went forth.

Forty-eight heaven seconds later and there, ahead, was his parents' house. Just as they had always wanted when they were alive. The wooden garden gate leading to a beautifully lawned front garden; hanging baskets were dotted around the house - and even a small orchard he could just see round the side. It warmed his heart knowing this. He strode forward and went to knock.

The demons were ready. Bob was ready. The Devil was ready. Zed's parents were ready to buy gas at any cost. The Angel was panicking and Zed was very drunk.

Chapter Sixty One

Spreading effortlessly, growing rapidly, blowing unobstructed, the great wind that now engulfed heaven was getting pissed off. Only the centre of heaven had resisted the unstoppable gallop of the wind and as far as the wind was concerned all should bow down and let it ride through. Skirting around the seemingly invisible barrier, the wind poked and probed for almost a day. Winds are well known for their stubbornness and their 'never-give-up' attitude. Only once they have puffed their last puff of energy do they say: "Right, time for a sleep." You will have seen this very moment yourself. The wind, full of strength, battering trees, blowing over bins and generally harassing anything in its path - and then nothing - instant relief from the wind. The rubbish drops to the floor, the trees regroup and the wind has gone to bed.

Well, this great wind still had plenty of puff. Like a dog seeing a cat through a small hole, the wind sensed a weakness in the shield. It ran head down, screaming a battle cry at the weakness, smashing against it. Most of the wind bounced off, egos dented and heads bruised. But some squeezed through. Rushing onwards, it did not wait for the rest of the mighty wind. Off it went, storming at trees that just a moment ago would have fallen from the wind's power but now nothing. Quite shocked that their, once powerful, energy had no effect on the ancient towering trees, it retreated. Feeling angry and embarrassed, it swirled around waiting for the rest of the wind to seep through.

The still-trapped remainder of the wind followed. Not in an orderly queue but in a mad turbulent frenzy. Slowly, more and more wind seeped through, heading for the centre. And at the centre they were focussing in on one target - Zed's parents' house.

Chapter Sixty Two

Shaking, partly from nerves but mainly from alcohol, Zed approached the door for the tenth time. At each attempt, his hand almost connected to produce an audible knock at the door but each time doubts brought the hand back. This was followed by a lot of pacing, working out what to say and attempting to talk himself into having yet another try.

Raising his hand fully, convinced this was the time, an eloquent and emotional greeting ready in the traps waiting to be released from his lips, he swung his arm down; picking up speed, it approached the door, doubts crawled out from where they had been beaten away. They shouted: "Stop, don't do it." "ABORT," ordered the brain. An order shouted too late. The hand would never stop in time. In sheer panic, Zed went to grab his hand with his other, throwing his weight forward, and at that very moment the advanced parties of the wind reached the house blowing the door open. Zed braced for his hand to impact on the door. Down the hand went, followed by his other that had now caught the first. Down they carried on going, past where the door had once stood solid but now was just air. His centre of gravity placed in an alarmingly unbalanced position gave in, he fell to the ground, head and torso in the house, with his legs still outside.

Blinded by confusion, Zed shouted for help, his voice muffled and silenced by the thick carpet his face found itself greeting. Regaining his senses and feeling ridiculous about his current position, he got to his feet and confidently said: "Hello." Followed by a slightly less confident: "Bit of a surprise, but it's me, Zed. Your son." The shock of the fall sobered Zed up in an impressively speedy manner.

Did he really need to mention the son part? He felt a bit silly. They won't have forgotten their son's named Zed, so no need to mention it. Oh well, it's done now.

No one replied so he shouted a bit louder. This time he heard a muffled response but couldn't work out the message. It kept shouting - or making a noise at least - so Zed followed the sound and with each few steps, the voices grew louder. Onwards through the living room, which he was pleased to see had pictures of himself as a wee baby dotted round the walls. No humans making strange noises, however. Up a flight of stairs he went, the noise growing louder, almost recognisable as his mother. His brain was not allowing for emotion as he gripped the doorknob and opened the door to the bathroom, and there in front of him lay his parents.

Joy, love and happiness rushed through his body, followed sharply by confusion. Why were his parents bound and gagged? A minute passed, filled mainly with Zed's mouth opening and shutting, unable to grasp what was going on. Staring from his dad, then to his mum both of whom were exasperated at their son, who seemed to be ignoring their desperate pleas for help. The brain, getting bored with constant messages from the mouth to open and shut, took control again sending a painfully clear signal to sort himself out. Zed snapping out of this daze ran to his mum, took off her gag and with doubts forgotten, and only happiness lingering in his mind, hugging his mother he said: "It's me mum."

"Oh Zed, how wonderful, you've come to rescue us. Quick, untie us. We need to escape the gas man."

That explains it, Zed decided. Gas man being over aggressive again. Strangely, or normally in Zed's own little world, he did not question their aggressive techniques further.

He untied his dad and mum, making mental note never to cross a gas salesman. The knots seemed overly tight and professionally tied for a salesman.

Never a family in life to physically embrace in order to show their family love, this moment took on an awkward air. Breaking through all their barriers, in each of the three humans, involved love. And the love you build from years of missing each other, fought through to demand an embrace. They hugged, a hug that would melt the heart of any passer by. Shaking off all their inhibitions, the hug felt right, it felt special.

Being the senior dad figure, Pete felt obliged to end this extraordinary moment in time to concentrate on perhaps a more pressing issue. "No time to explain," Pete said, "we need to get out of here before they come back."

And perhaps, if Zed had remembered his boyhood knot untying techniques from scouts, they could have fled.

Demons you see are lazy. Demogorgen felt his patrolling ability dwarfed his fellow demons. The other three had all fallen asleep while on watch and here he was, wide awake, sprung ready for action - or at least that's what it felt like in his dream. As five minutes earlier, deciding to take a seat, having paced for over two minutes, he'd drifted off into a deep, snoring sleep. It was just a shame he was now awake and outside the bathroom door, alert and feeling decidedly evil with the other three demons all in similar states of minds.

Cackling, witch-like, all four barged their way into the family reunion. "And where the fuck do you think you maggots are going?"

Zed's brain fought for an answer - four, disgusting, monster-like humanoids needed rationalising - and quick. Being a lazy brain and not wanting to overthink the situation - partly also out of a lack of clever ideas - the decision was made to reuse an old technique, and assume these four were in fancy dress. Never mind why.

While the brain was off rationalising things hurriedly, the normally quiet part took the rare opportunity to be heard. This was the unused brain receptor. Taking Zed by surprise, he summoned up all his courage and confronted these intruders. "Look, sirs or madams, my mum and dad have made it perfectly clear they do not require gas. Do you comprehend? Now kindly leave, else I will report you to your seniors."

"Is this guy for real? This can't be the one the boss is obsessed about. I thought he'd be fucking special, muscles bursting from every orifice, head twice the size of them normal shitty ones humans have. He's just a dick."

Still with some power, the brave part of Zed's brain carried on. "Why is your boss obsessed by me? I have only been in heaven a few days and just want to be left alone with my parents please."

"Yeah sure, shit face. We'll leave you alone with them." The demons looked at one another smiling, knowing they would have time to tease and play with their captors. "You can all be alone together in hell when the boss gets here. Hey, Crocell, when's he coming?"

Answering the question less in words than actions, things started to happen. Not a ring on the phone nor knock at the door, not even a shout from outside. Satan doesn't do those sorts of things; he has his own special ways.

At that moment the room started vibrating. Richter scale 'Devil', some seismologists (or earthquakeologists for a more pleasing name) would declare. Windows flexed in an impossible dance, climaxing in a shattering encore, as they smashed one by one, spraying glass across the floor. A deafening noise came from below howling and screaming, not in fear more in anger. The bath taps shot out water without the taps being on and in the corner the toilet started to behave in a highly peculiar manner. No one noticed at first the smoke seeping out from the closed toilet seat. The pressure building underneath it started lifting it up and down, bellowing out more and more smoke until finally, shooting out like steam from a high pressure cooker, everyone turned and watched the once unnoticed white, plain, close-coupled, porcelain toilet. With an eruption of water copied straight from an upside down Niagara Falls, sewage shot up and out from the toilet, taking the seat and impaling it into the ceiling. The room was now shaking, full of smoke – and it stank!

To many a Devil worshipper, this scene may seem fitting for the Lord of the underworld, a heroic entrance they would say, not so the Devil himself.

Head and horns sticking out, the Devil momentarily appeared stuck before hauling himself out, flopping onto the floor in a beached whale-like manner.

Getting up off the newly rancid floor, coughing and spluttering, he ran for the now open (lacking glass) window and was violently sick. This was not the entrance he had intended. His new pristine, expertly fitted suit was now covered in crap and his shoes were ruined.

"Who the fuck chose to put the hell hole in the fucking toilet?" The demons pointed at Crocell, eager to snitch and avoid what would come. Staring in a more composed manner, the Devil eyeballed Crocell. "You my friend shall spend eternity living in the U bend of hell's toilet."

"No master, I beg you. I just thought it was true to the scriptures that you, my Lord, should rise from the bowels of hell."

"You thought wrong." He clicked his finger and the demon was gone, he clicked them again and he now wore a new suit and shoes, clean suit and shoes that is. Not the ones he had wanted - but they would do.

He regained his composure and introduced himself.

"Apologies for my entrance, lady and gentlemen. I am the Devil, ruler of the underworld and I come to make you an offer. I would like you, Zed, to come and live in hell." Not wasting time, he had got straight to the point.

Zed's draw dropped. His brain was trying to hide not wanting to be involved. So Zed just stared.

"You see Zed, I know you don't fit in round here. All this walking for a start. In hell we have cars and pubs every ten metres. I know hell has a bad rep but honestly, and trust me Zed when I say this, it's like a dream come true living down there."

Agares sniggered and said: "Yeah a dream come true, if you like pain and fire and probes stuck where the sun don't shine."

"Quiet you imbecile!" And he clicked his finger once again, vanishing yet another demon.

"So just to be clear," Zed enquired. "You are the Devil?"

"Yes."

"And you would like me to come hell with you?"

"Yes. But hell is such an old name. We call it 'Funland' now."

The two remaining demons sniggered but instantly stopped as their boss threw them a stare that threatened death with one click.

"Are these your gas men?"

"Yes, I mean what? Gas men? Look, will you come to Funland and enjoy our hospitality?"

"Well, thank you for your offer but I am here with my parents so am going to stay. And also we will be complaining about your gas sellers too. Pointing at the toilet Zed said: "And if you don't mind, could you all leave."

It was the Devil's mouth that dropped to the floor this time. "Is he really speaking to me like that? He's just a shorty, normal human and I'm the Devil." For one pico point in time he went to turn and go back below.

Sensing it was required, Zed's more commonly used part of the brain came out of hiding for a second and whispered to Zed: "You do know you're talking to the Devil?" Zed heard this loud and clear. Now comprehending that the Devil was standing before him, he ran petrified and hid behind his parents.

The Devil also snapped back to himself. Wiping away that pico of a nano second in time, where he went to obey Zed, he puffed his clean-shaven, shining red chest with a deep breath, filling his lungs with the raging wind, appeared to grow twice his size and roared a roar that would take a thousand lions a million years to generate. "You speak to me like that you fuck face? I'm going to torture you for eternity and then torture you some more." Always one for details, he carried on in a voice that was followed by a rush of air stretching the skin on Zed's face backwards, like five Gs of force. "I'm going to pull your eyes out with boiling hot chopsticks, make you eat them and then replace them with what comes out the other end. You'll then be seeing shit as well as talking it. Get them, demons. Drag them down to our kingdom, pull their tongues out if they scream, rip their arms off if they resist!"

Excited like a pack of dogs, the two remaining demons frothed at the mouth eager to do their boss's evil bidding. As the demons approached menacingly, the bathroom door flew off its hinges and smashed on the wall opposite.

"In the name of the law and Lord, I banish you to hell. Now be gone!"

Turning more in annoyance than fear, the demons and the Devil looked at the party pooper interrupting their work. "Oh look lads, it's Elemiah. Why are you here, for fuck sake? Go back to whatever you were doing. Weren't you good at singing? Can't remember you ever being good at fighting."

The Devil stared at Elemiah in a face of pure contempt.

"I am here to stop whatever you are doing."

"What's that then?"

"Well, bad stuff, why don't you tell me?"

"We're just here on a peaceful, fact-finding, relationship-building mission - honest."

Turning her attitude a few notches towards the aggressive, she persisted: "Tell me what you are up to!"

She had missed seeing Zed enter the house - as even Angels need sleep. The vibrations and noise from the Devil's entrance woke her from her slumbers and after quickly sorting out her hair she rushed in to save the day.

"Oh no, not a tiny, weeny, embarrassing excuse for an Angel. Please don't hurt us." Turning to his demons the Devil said: "Is that really the best old man God can do to protect his heaveners? If I were Him, I'd have sent an army. But no, he's always on about not interfering and peaceful negotiations."

Elemiah seized upon this sentence. "There is an army of Angels on their way." She said firmly and thought "I hope."

"Oh well, we surrender then. Eek, should we just wait around here until they turn up? Or perhaps we'll fucking finish the job before they get here."

"Excuse me," Zed's mum said having politely listened for the last ten minutes. "But why do you want my son? Did he not lead a good life and was gifted with his key to heaven?"

"Ah, I thought no one would ask." The Devil took on the tone of a businessman instead of his evil Devil persona and addressed the room. "Many millennia ago, me and God had this little disagreement. One thing led to another and I became the Devil and hell became my kingdom. I was pretty happy with the outcome. I was King, Lord and leader. I could do what I wanted. But then God started sending humans there. He knew I hated humans and so, in response, I tortured them. These people were the worst of the worst, so even God thought they deserved it. Well that kept me amused for a while; but the trickle of people through the years has turned into a never-ending swarm of disgusting humans that are packed into my land. Hell became overcrowded and it has become not only their hell, but mine as well. I know He did this on purpose, sitting up there, all smug for thousands of years, knowing that one day hell would be my worst nightmare. So I've had enough."

"Hah, I knew it. You've come up here to take heaven by force. No Angel will rest until you are defeated, no human will...."

"Oh shut up, Elemiah. I am not here to overthrow heaven with an army of demons. Now where was I? The mistake God made was sending the clever ones down. Evil geniuses. I have thousands of them. Each new hell arrivee is given a test. If they pass, then they join my planning team. An infinite amount of monkeys, over eternity would one day write the entire works of Shakespeare, but I only needed thousands of geniuses and hundreds of years. I set them a task. Find a way for me to go back to heaven, and you, Zed, you are my way." The Devil's huge red finger pointed squarely at Zed's head.

A brief silence was quickly filled with the demons applauding, always keen to please their boss.

"Sorry, but it must be all a mistake. I'm just Zed. So please leave." Zed still crouched behind his parents, had a tone more of begging than authority.

"Get up Zed," said his father "where's your stiff upper lip?"

"Sorry dad."

This instruction jolted Zed into remembering why he was here.

"Mum, dad why do you not want me here?"

"What do you mean dear?" replied his confused mum.

"I was told by a fortune reader that when I arrived here, you and dad would be angry and not have any interest in me staying."

"Don't be stupid son. We have been counting down our estimated day until your arrival. We had plans to come and find you once we were sure you'd passed away. Your mum and I yearned for this day. And now this red baboon has ruined it."

"That's splendid news. I'm over the moon. And this pesky curse must also have been lifted." Zed, somehow forgetting all the other current terrors, smiled, pleased he was no longer cursed, remembering they had hugged earlier.

His dad, now a bit angry asked: "Curse, us hating you, fortune tellers? You been taking them drug things, son?"

Elemiah butted in: "I can explain all Zed but for now let's deal with the issues in front of us. You know, the Devil and that?"

"You two finished your father son crap yet, so I can carry on? Good. Now shut up and listen."

One arm behind his back, Napoleon style, Satan walked around the room while talking. "For the last seven thousand years, each morning I've heard a new plan on how to get back up here. Most were so shit I made them eat their plan and then eat it again when it came out."

"Out of where?" asked Zed's mum.

"Out their fucking arse hole you inbred idiot, where else?!"

"That's grotesque," said Zed's mum, deeply offended.

The Devil smiled. "I know," staring disturbingly straight at her face.

"Occasionally, they brought plans that at first glance seemed perfect. But there was always a flaw. The ex-army, fuck-wit majors that I have to put up with are always planning a war; but what's the point in that? A war would trash heaven and then it would be just as shitty as it is in hell. I was almost at the point of giving up when I was presented with this plan. I was amazed at how simple it was, and then fucking angry that the douche bag geniuses took fucking forever to think of it. You see, hell is the detachment of God's love. A detachment of God's love! There, it was written in some crappy religious scripture. To go to hell means God has disowned you; he's put you in a bag and thrown you in the river."

"So what," said Elemiah. "God doesn't love them because they have lived a life of hate and evil. They have wasted the life God gave them and so he cuts them loose. The amount of chances God gives them through their life? But no, they choose to waste them."

"Yes, and he discards all his crap on me. I'm his fucking sewer and this sewer rat is staking a claim to a nice house up here. Getting back to the plan. Every person who ever came to hell was meant to be there, not one person came by mistake. But now Zed, now you are coming.

"Why?" questioned Elemiah, "how will that help you?"

"Because it will make hell impossible to exist. You know heaven and hell are not made by the crappy rules that God defined earth with. If something is said in the scriptures that came from God then that is the truth. To break the truth would mean the truth was never there."

"Sorry boss for interrupting but why didn't we just grab somebody and bring them to heaven? And why did we try so hard to stop him seeing his parents?"

"A sensible question for once from a demon. Miracles do fucking happen. The parents bit is easy. I don't give a toss that Zed met his parents. All I needed was a way to make the Angels and God notice I was up to something. I know God knew I was double bluffing, but I was bluffing on something else. To kidnap and take someone down to hell would not work. No, for this to be powerful enough to reverse hell, it needs witnesses. God must see and Angels must talk, as truth is only true if people are there to tell the story. It grows and grows in power the more it is talked about and repeated. Does a falling tree make a sound if nothing is there to hear it?"

Zed's Dad, not thinking, butted in: "Well, yes it does, as sound is purely pressure waves and these would be created by the fall, regardless of witnesses."

"Shut up or I'll stick a Zimmer frame up your old-man arse." Adjusting his suit to gain some composure he continued. "As I said, heaven does not obey stupid earth rules. When God sees me take his child to hell, it will cause hell to disappear and I will be returned to heaven. One of God's children will be down in hell; it can't happen. Hell's definition is void. If there are enough witnesses and rumours and talk besides, there will be enough power to accomplish this geniusly simple plan." Grinning, the Devil gestured with a hand movement that his presentation was complete.

Zed, summoning a bit of courage asked: "But why me?"

Walking up to Zed, lifting him up in the air by his top and breathing his foul smelling breath inches from Zed's face he said: "Because you are a dick head. Or more importantly in God's eyes, you are the pinnacle of his crappy human race. You are average and have gone through life, not excelling, but just getting through it. You've done nothing very bad and not really been noticed. To God, you are perfect."

"Oh." Zed didn't know if this was an insult or compliment but in his current state of terror, he didn't particularly care.

"Well I can't see God watching you and apart from us few, no one will see. So your plan will fail. Now go back to hell and stop this ridiculous scene." Elemiah was stalling for time in the tiny hope a miracle would happen.

"I will, don't worry. I will be returning to hell as soon as I get Zed." And with lightning speed he grabbed Zed hoisted him over his shoulder and went to leave.

Outside someone shouted: "Stop!!!"

The Devil smiled. People should worry when the Devil smiles. Popping Zed - remarkably carefully for an ogre like brute of a beast - onto the once clean, cream lino floor, he went to see who was making all the racket. For it was not just a solidarity voice but a wave of sound from an ocean of voices.

Cath, Pete and Elemiah leaned out of a smashed window. And there, looking the most handsome and heroic he had ever mustered up - which still registered on the low scale – was Bob. And behind him were several thousand followers all packed together into a blur of crazed Zed fans. If anyone looked more closely they'd see an impressive collection of humans from different countries, religions and times, all mixed and shaken into a collective following.

The crowd were starting to chant. "We want Zed. We want Zed." Some shouted with just as much vigour and passion: "Grunt, grunt , grunt."

Bob at the front of them all raised his hand for silence. "Behold the chosen one. Come forth our great saviour Zed."

Pete mumbled, mainly to himself, about how they had ruined his lawn; and who was going to pay for all the lovingly grown vegetables that now were invisible under the pounding of Zed's people.

Zed, who was just picking himself up off the floor, entered a state he was used to - complete confusion and stumbled to the window to look out.

The crowd drew a deep breath - and then silence.

Having travelled day and night to hear the great Zed speak, some no doubt, were disappointed that the Devil took the initiative first. "You fools, you come to save this little squirming maggot? I could crush him in one move if I wanted."

A well-versed follower from the crowd shouted out: "But it is foretold that a great army of good will save the brave Zed from evil. We will fight you and win." A deafening cheer erupted. If Zed had the nature or desire to become a powerful leader, he would have grabbed the euphoria of the frenzied crowd and made an historic, spirit-lifting speech. Instead he heroically stood doing nothing.

Elemiah, sensing that she should seize the momentum herself, flew out the windows and hovered above Zed's great army. Although he knew nothing about his army, it was still nevertheless his.

"Look at the power God has. In just a few days an army has been formed to fight you. Just imagine how many will join. Following swiftly behind them an army of Angels will arrive to banish you back to hell. That's if you are lucky, as this time God might not be so generous." Elemiah flew upwards in a spiral hoping to impress the army and bring them courage but more importantly, to try to see if any Angels were on their way.

"Look boys," the Devil said to the demons. "A fucking army is here to stop us. We should surrender now. Wave the white flag, put our hands up high."

"We should? But boss I reckon we could take them."

"Oh for fuck sake," the Devil muttered under his breath. "No I was being sarcastic!" And he swung round extending his arm and pointed directly at Bob. "Attack!"

The two remaining demons ran at the wall of the house and smashed straight through. In hell it had taken hundreds of years and many rebuilt buildings until demons understood doors could be opened and did not require smashing. Landing on the floor they stopped, looked at the army of Bob, and screamed a deathly roar.

The army all took a step back in unison, but Bob stood firm. Turning to his (or Zed's army) he spoke. "Do not be afraid. We can defeat anything." He walked up to the first demon and swung a punch. It was the sort of punch you'd see from an ageing granny who was not very good at punching. It barely touched the demon; it struggled even to part the air particles as it went through, yet the demon went down screaming. Bob turned to the crowd, a glazed look in his eyes and fist held high. "Behold my magic strength."

Elemiah still hovering flew back in and faced the Devil. She knew something was wrong, a minute ago she was convinced this army would protect Zed and stop the Devil's evil plan - or at least delay his plan while the demons destroyed them. But now doubt was creeping – creeping like a tidal wave – into her mind. She was not so sure and was getting worried.

"What have you done? Why did your crony demon go down to a human's punch? Not even a punch, more a flick. He hardly touched him."

"You'll see, fairy girl."

Walking to the window again he shouted out to Bob: "You are strong and possess powers of greatness. Will you join me?"

The crowd again were stunned. Some even laughed. Join the Devil? Don't be stupid!

Elemiah was overloading on panic juice. She knew the Devil must have planned this whole thing, but what could she do? She was no match for the Devil and although humans couldn't die, the Devil could kill her. The other Angels would not come. They thought she was mad.

"We will fight you to the end!" cried someone from the crowd.

Lost in a cloud of thoughts, Zed was staring at Bob. Here was the mad man who had briefly met him and somehow summoned thousands of followers to defend him from the Devil. Not normally inclined to swear, he allowed a brief moment of anger to erupt from his thoughts and shouted out: "What the feck. Why is this happening? I'm Zed. Everyone just leave me alone." Remembering his dad was present and his manners he added: "I mean, please, could everyone disperse and leave me with my family."

Still staring at Bob, Zed could see the manic look in his eyes. Almost a blank look, one that stares right through you as though you were not there. Like you were so insignificant that you did not deserve to obstruct his view.

It was Bob's turn to speak. Climbing up onto a lovingly built garden wall he shouted. "Oh bollocks." Re climbing onto the wall and this time sitting to avoid falling off he continued. "I have told you all of this day. The day we rescue the chosen one from evil. But my friends we were wrong."

A huge intake of breath by everyone in the crowd was quickly followed by people looking at each other - and confusion reigned.

"This," pointing at Zed, "this is the evil one. He has plans to destroy us all; plans so disgustingly grotesque, I will not darken your dreams with the details. The Devil or Lucifer as we will know him needs rescuing from Zed. If Zed is not taken to hell as punishment then heaven will perish and so will we."

No one cheered.

"But you said Zed was our saviour," a more inquisitive member of the crowd pointed out.

"Yes, I sort of got it a bit wrong. (Minor details and all that). The greatest men amongst us will not be shy when admitting their mistakes."

"What about the women? Do the greatest women also admit to their mistakes?" shouted a annoyed, confident woman.

Losing his train of thought for a moment Bob answered. "Yes, them too."

"Then why say the men? I mean, is it so hard to say people? I'm tempted to report this to the Equal Rights of Zed's Army Union you know."

Understanding the power of unions, Bob relented. "I take back my terrible mistake and am announcing I will be going on an 'Equal Rights For All' course. Furthermore, I would like it known that some of my best friends are women." This seemed to appease the hormonal woman. (The writer of this book would like it known some of his best friends are (or were) women....)

Bob, taking a second to remember where he was in his heroic speech, carried on. "Lucifer is here to wash the evil out of heaven. He guards us from them. He is not to be afraid of; think of him as the prison chief protecting us, wrapping the blanket of safety around us all. I know this, as I am Special. Did you not just see the miracle performed? I, a mere human, defeated a demon."

Muttered sounds of approval arose from the crowd. "And look at this, I have brought Lucifer here to banish Zed, the evil one, from heaven." He spoke in a tone that crowds love. Once you get a few in a crowd on your side, the ripple effect can be equated to heroine. No one can resist it once they have been exposed. The approval started to be heard with clapping crescendoing into cheers and then chants of: "Zed out. Bob to lead."

Elemiah was so angry, her emotions flung her into a rage. Flying at the Devil, she pushed him with the force of an elephant. A human would now be splattered against the nearest wall, yet on the Devil it had no effect. He stayed motionless with his arms crossed above his chest. "Why has he done this? He was just an idiot who got the wrong idea about Zed and now he has turned to your side," she shouted, fists pounding in the Devil's chest in frustration.

"Power. Power is a drug humans cannot resist. He has been taking the power drug ever since he won his first follower. With each new one the drug became more addictive. The feeling of commanding people to follow Zed, instructing them where to go, what to wear and where to eat was amazing. But then, like all greedy humans, he thought: "Why are they not following me? I created this yet they only respect Zed." He became bitter and twisted which attracted my attention. I knew he was raising an army of followers and they would be a minor annoyance to me. But I saw a way to flip the coin in my favour. I offered him more power, greater control and of course women - as all dumb men have their weaknesses. I told him he could be the leader and without much effort, he got into bed with me. Not only did I get the people here I needed, to make the truth real, but I also had an army just in case pesky Angels turned up. But they didn't believe you, did they? Well enough of this rubbish."

The Devil turned back to the crowd. "Bob has commanded me to do this. Risking his life, he brought me here to take Zed down below to God's great prison. The inescapable fire of doom where all damned souls eventually go to rot. Trickery, lies and sorcery deceived poor old Peter to open the gates and now I'm here to drag him to where he belongs. If anyone tries to stop me, attack them for they are helping evil."

"We will," shouted Bob

"We will," echoed the army.

Chillingly, the Devil gave Elemiah a wink. "Come now Zed, you will release me back to heaven. Enough people have witnessed this momentous event. God will know and the story will grow."

Zed tried to run but fear had fused his legs stiff. In desperation he closed his eyes and wished. Some would call it praying but to Zed it was a wish.

He felt the Devil's huge ice-cold hand on his shoulder. If there was one time in his existence that Zed needed a plan it was now, but his brain was locked in the castle's keep, drawbridge up and stocked with food for months and had no intentions of coming out.

Watching helplessly, his mum and dad held hands, weeping. All was lost for Zed. All was won for the Devil.

He picked Zed up and made his way over to the toilet.

"We going back now boss?" asked a demon as they both jumped effortlessly up through the first floor window.

"Yes, but not down that fucking shit hole. Now make me another hell door that isn't covered in crap."

"Yes boss."

"And make it quick. Death by nuclear bomb quick."

With only two demons left, forming a chanting circle proved impossible. The less traditional line was formed instead. This time, with the boss present, they knelt on their knees, hands straight above their heads. Rhythmically moving up and down they started their chanting - one humming while the other screamed.

In science, they call it a step change, not something that gradually grows or even something that quickly happens. It's a change that is instantaneous, from being one thing it's suddenly something else, with no in between 'getting to know one another' in the middle. This is what happened to the air around and in Zed's parents' home.

But as the demons chanted, the wind slam-dunked its way in, brushing away the smashed glass and smashing it yet further into smithereens against the interior bathroom wall. All the humans stumbled from the force of the wind and grabbed hold of the nearest thing they could. In Zed's case it was the Devil – who he quickly let go of – in fear.

Outside the house, looking up high in the sky there was not a scene of heroic Angels rushing to save the day. Instead, circling round, powered by the energy of every wind to ever exist, the great wind, accompanied by black, light destroying clouds, swirled a dance of destruction around the house. Directly above was a small circle of blue sky light pouring through, rushing in before the route would be blocked as the circle got smaller and smaller. People were running for cover, the clouds didn't rain water - they rained panic. Above the noise people screamed at Bob demanding answers.

"What is this wind Bob? It's going to kill us all?" And many more went for the traditional: "Help!"

Bob, with his crazed madman eyes shouted above the wind: "This is the Power. Look what we control."

Only the demons, Bob and the Devil remained calm. Elemiah, now in a complete panic looked at the horizon. All around was a wall of wind. Carrying chairs, trees, humans and more, it battered anything in its path. "Oh bugger," she thought, "the Devil is going to destroy heaven if he takes Zed to hell."

She went right up to the Devil and screamed above the noise of the wind. "Can't you see what you are doing? If you take Zed you will destroy heaven and hell. You are going against the word of God," she pleaded.

"You fool, this is the power - it is happening. It's the start of wiping away my banishment and hell. Heaven will still be here and I will be in it. It's because so many eyes have witnessed what will happen to Zed."

"You're wrong. Stop it now."

The wind had now spread from the far corners (if there are corners in heaven) to the very centre of Zed's parents' house. It was circling its prey. It engulfed the army, swallowing thousands of the followers at once, funnelling them up and spitting them out so they scattered in all directions, landing with great thuds on the floor. Left on his own, Bob was commanding it to stop, still thinking he had ultimate power over the wind. The wind laughed and leapt forward gobbling him up, throwing him so high in the sky that Bob reached heights even Angels cannot fly too.

Only the house was left.

Inside the badly damaged bathroom the noise resembled Earth on creation day. Ignoring everything, the Devil was still beaming with happiness. He knew the plan was working, the truth had grown in power and now was the time to climax.

"Have you finished the door or do you need some gentle if painful encouragement?"

"Yes sire, it is ready."

"Let's get out of this shit hole then."

Elemiah grabbed Zed, Pete took hold of Elemiah and Cath grabbed Pete. They pulled as hard as they could. But the Devil with one effortless movement snatched Zed and commanded his demons. "Go now."

A few days ago the wind was quite calm but with strength it grew angry. Rage had gripped its senses blinding it and it had forgotten its manners. Rushing head first down through heaven it had destroyed homes, razed forests and ruined farms; but now on reaching the final destination, it remembered. No longer confused, it knew why it felt so angry. Spinning faster than heavenly possible, the wind started to form a point. Like an arm in the spinning wind, it reached out probing, searching the room.

The Devil turned, confident he knew what was going on. He was calm with the situation under control. Then from the corner of his fire-stained eye he noticed the point. The calm collapsed, rage replaced the space and he felt sick. For he knew what was happening. "Oh fuck!"

The wind grabbed the Devil. Smashed him against all four walls and dragged him towards the toilet.

"Nooo. You will not win!" he shouted looking wildly around him. "Get me, demons. Release me from this thing." They moved but were instantly picked up by the wind, pinning them against the bathroom wall.

"How have you done this? You bastard." Grabbing air frantically the Devil manically attempted to escape.

The wind didn't like this sort of talk, and Elemiah, holding desperately to the doorframe, could have sworn it said: "Be gone." And with that the Devil and all the demons were thrown back down the toilet. Not one at a time - they all went down headfirst - together. Technically speaking that was impossible, but again, in heaven, technically does not get to have its say often.

Chapter Sixty Three

Down below, the Devil gazed vacantly at his soiled suit and ruined shoes. He didn't bother changing them though. With shoulders drooping, head hung low and feet dragging, he walked off back to his home. He was too depressed to even have a go at the demons or punish the people who created his great plan. All he had wanted was a little home in heaven where he could relax. Why could God not forgive him? Just because he had tricked God into wiping out almost everything with that Noah's ark practical joke that went wrong - and the other little things he had been accused of over the years. He would have his revenge one day; but for now he required sleep and lots of it. Maybe for a year or ten. With all the executives, project managers and so-called leaders down here, hell could manage itself these days.

Chapter Sixty Four

The wind retreated following its path of destruction. No longer angry, it undid the damage unfurled in its wake. A lone angel watching above witnessed it all, as normality returned to Zed's home. Lingering for a while, he saw the beauty of a family re-united as they sipped a summer cocktail in their garden and talked of this and that. None of this really made any impression on the Angel though. Turning round to fly home, he muttered under his breath: "I knew it! No bloody tea. She promised tea."

Chapter Sixty Five

The butterfly, having braved the wind and ridden its turbulent waves through heaven, had witnessed the saga unfold below. It smiled. A smile cannot be seen very easily on a butterfly, but it was there. Nothing made the butterfly happier than seeing a loving family; that was why it had gone to all this trouble. Humans, it thought to himself, are amazing. They do such stupid things and ask ever increasingly ridiculous questions - but it still loved them. I mean, why are they so obsessed by riddles like the chicken and egg; always banging on about which came first?

The answer is, of course, the chicken - by a good hundred years. It was only because God grew so annoyed when humans started eating them that he created the egg - and then they started eating eggs too. They do like to test God's patience.

One day he would send another Son down to earth to answer this great question. Or maybe a daughter this time. Fluttering off, the butterfly hummed a favourite tune it had heard from a human. If you listened carefully you may just hear what sounded like.

'I'm on the highway to hell....'

The End

To leave a review please follow the below link. Rewards (bribes) for good reviews can be collected upon reaching heaven.

https://www.amazon.co.uk/Its-Hell-Up-Heaven-Austin-ebook/dp/B01G2MJSKW

Follow J S Austin on Twitter at https://twitter.com/jsaustin666

21120222R00134

Printed in Great Britain
by Amazon